THE INHUMAN RACE

YUDHANJAYA WIJERATNE was born in Ratnapura, Sri Lanka, and grew up in Colombo, writing about local technology and politics on the controversial Icaruswept blog. He has written and edited Readme.lk, Sri Lanka's first tech journalism network, and his work has appeared in The *Sunday Times, The Sunday Observer, The Nation, Sunday Leader, The Colombo Telegraph* and *Groundviews*. His first two science fiction works, *Numbercaste* and *The Slow Sad Suicide of Rohan Wijeratne*, were published in 2017. He is currently a researcher with the Big Data Team at LIRNEasia, a non-profit think tank that works across Asia, Africa and the Pacific Islands.

THE INHUMAN RACE

YUDHANJAYA WIJERATNE

HarperCollins *Publishers* India

First published in India by
HarperCollins *Publishers* in 2018

Building 10, Tower A, 4th Floor, DLF Cyber City, Phase II,
Gurugram Haryana – 122002, India
www.harpercollins.co.in

2 4 6 8 10 9 7 5 3 1

P-ISBN: 978-93-5302-331-7
E-ISBN: 978-93-5302-332-4

This is a work of fiction and all characters and incidents described in this book are the product of the author's imagination. Any resemblance to actual persons, living or dead, is entirely coincidental.

Typeset in 11/14 Scala (OTF) at
Manipal Digital Systems, Manipal

Printed and bound at
MicroPrints India, New Delhi

To those Time took: Terry Pratchett, Ursula Le Guin, Phillip K. Dick, and J.M. Barrie. Your stories gave light to a dark childhood.

ONE

It was night.

A pale and sickly moon hung over the darkness of Colombo, Ceylon. Spires, many of them old, shell-blasted hotels, reached out to the sky. They made shapes in the skyline: A, B, C – black silhouettes on gray.

The Union Jack flew over the city, blue-black in the darkness, and just below it, flapping slightly in the wind, hung a flag with a yellow lion on it.

'The Bluetooth device is ready to pair,' a voice blared, shattering the awful darkness.

The little girl sat up with, jolted from her sleep, her mouth frozen in a soundless scream.

'The Bluetooth device has connected successfully,' announced the voice. It had a slight Chinese accent.

And now, through the night came the sound of a drumbeat, low and stealthy; it soon gave way to the high and melodic strains of violins. It was Max Bruch's first concerto in G minor, although in this world, they just knew it as the Music that did not kill.

The girl relaxed. Bleary eyes misted over with sleep, she curled up again and pulled the tarpaulin over herself. Outside, the soul of a dead German composer played itself out in the warm, rotting air, violins keening to a city that no longer knew what a violin was.

≈

It was Monday when she woke again. She knew it was Monday because the radio said 7.30 A.M. MONDAY.

Mondays were important. She packed up the radio with great care and gathered the rest of her things. A cloak cut of shiny green plastic. Her spear – a simple steel tube with 'Galle Face Hotel' stamped on the side. One edge was wrapped in cloth, the other had been sharpened to a spike. Finally, the bag. She set off awkwardly, her plastic backpack clanking softly. The only other sound was that of the crows, screaming their councils over the rot and the decay.

It was windy outside. The Galle Face breeze played over the slow sea, over burned-out shells of towers. It touched the great garbage mountain that leaned against the tallest of these towers, a rotting corpse supported by a steel-and-glass crucifix, blotting out whatever horizon lay beyond. Its base, cordoned off by rusted, broken barriers, stretched for almost a mile in every direction. A slow sea wrapped itself around both the mountain and the land that stretched out from under its putrid feet.

≈

At the turn of the 5th century, a young monk – called Fa-Xian by himself, Fa-Hien by others – walked the early Silk Roads all the way from China to India to this little island of Ceylon, searching for the great Buddhist texts. Two years he had stayed here before he sailed back to his home country, where he then spent the rest of his life translating the scriptures he had found on his travels. He died at the ripe old age of eighty-eight in the great Monastery of Sin, having spread the word of the Buddha and set the stage for much bloodshed to come.

Many thousands of years later, the first Song Emperor, having won the might of a united China, brooded over his navy from his darkened throne room. The white devils that flew the Union Jack ruled too much of the ocean for his liking. Dimly, he remembered Fa-Xian's accounts of Ceylon, the Buddha's blessed island that also seemed of such value to ships traversing those seas, and with one imperious wave of his hand the Song Emperor dispatched ten of his finest ships to see what could be done.

And thus the British Empire's first direct contact with China in two hundred years was when the Chinese warships pulled up to the Colombo port and began their assault. The then-Governer, drinking high tea at Galle Face, cried out in alarm as a 10-kilo warhead wiped out most of his office. The next second it exploded, blowing the man, his staff, and ten thousand other people into so much dust in the air.

By the time the battle ended, the port city of Colombo lay in ruins. Buildings lay strewn about like matchsticks. Blood and molten metal ran in the streets and mixed. Lakes broke their boundaries, flooded, then boiled over.

A British Tin Soldier lay smoking on the battlefield, its railgun-arms blasted clean out of their sockets, its operator a charred and broken heap of flesh inside.

The two remaining Chinese ships took back terms from the Queen: the British Empire was glad to conduct business with Great China, and would grant them permission to build their own port here in Ceylon, if they agreed to a treaty of peace and commerce.

Colombo? A diplomatic incident, nothing more.

'Peace,' offered Elizabeth, who was sometimes called Iron Lizzie on the streets.

The Song Emperor nodded from the darkness

'Peace,' he replied, and the deed was done. The British retreated warily. The Chinese terraformers advanced with equal caution. The British East India Trading Company, docking at the new port city, offered silver and art, and the Chinese responded with silks and tea.

And between them, as the price of progress, lay a no-man's land where there had once been a city, a graveyard where warped ruins cast strange shadows under the hot sun.

≈

Through this mess, now moved a little girl with a makeshift spear, tiny against the bones of the buildings that surrounded her. She walked slowly but steadily, with the flip-flop of slippers on what had once been a proper road. She came to the sea – what they had once called the Galle Face Green. That was when it had been a grass front facing the sea, and had played host to couples on cheap dates and Nanas restaurants every five meters – each proudly claiming to be the original, the one and only true Nanas – 'come sir come, kotthu, fried-rice, roast-chicken, Coke.'

But then the bombs had arrived, and Galle Face Green became Galle Face Brown, just a strip of pavement doing nothing in particular. Now it had no color worth speaking of.

The girl joined a mass of children who sat and stood and squatted here, forming a line of clanking, complaining bodies that moved slowly in the hot sun. In front of them was the entrance to the Port City. It was a looming gate with two fierce Buddhist guardians carved into stone and a platoon of men with body armor and guns backing them up. There was a truck parked just outside these gates, with harried-looking people in black bodysuits and power armor handing out packets and bags and boxes to the children.

'Next!' called a voice.

'Eelanga!' said another. 'Atutta! Xià yigè!'

The line of children shifted up by one, responding to their names. The little girl padded in that direction.

'Halt!' screeched three boys. They brandished cruel-looking knives. 'Colombo 3?'

She nodded.

'Ko identity?'

She dutifully turned over one of the badges she wore. A rough red 3 was painted there. The boys relaxed. The little girl joined the line.

'Kaawada?' asked the boy in front of her. *Have you eaten?*

Brown skin, darker at the forehead. A face that could be ten. Eyes that could be thirty.

She looked into those eyes and shook her head.

He pulled out a red packet of fuel biscuits from somewhere, counted three of them very carefully, and held them out to her. His eyes roamed over her little body, resting on the spear, the bag, the slippers. He pointed to the slippers.

She shook her head.

He snorted, added one more biscuit. Now there were four.

She looked at the biscuits with longing and shook her head again.

He shrugged and turned back to the line. 'It's going to take a long time,' he said, his voice nasal and metallic, cracked by long years of dust and sea-salt.

It did. When she finally got to the top of the line, she took a deep breath and held up the bag. The woman at the counter smiled. They knew each other. The Silent girl upended the bag. Out came a motley collection of cans and bottles – some of them still with their stickers on. These were swiftly carted away.

The girl held up the Radio and pressed a button.

'Food for two, please,' the Radio crackled.

The woman's smile fell. 'Oh, I'm sorry,' she whispered, her hands flitting over packages. 'Not enough food now, cannot give usual. Only one.'

The girl frowned. She pressed the button again, 'Food for two, please,' the Radio repeated insistently.

'Sorry!' said the woman at the counter. She pressed a box into the girl's hands. 'Is all I can give now. More food, now you bring me more cans. Next!'

The girl walked home slowly, slippers flip-flop-flapping on the asphalt. Several times they came for her, children with wild faces and knives, but each time she swung her metal, and each time they backed away. But she walked faster now. Galle Face was open ground – too open, unsafe.

It became better further down, where the automated gun guarded the old President's house. The corpse of a single child, its body shredded by machine gun fire, hung impaled on the gate. Sparks leaped from it occasionally.

She slipped across the road, carefully avoiding the firing arcs, until she came to her tower. It was a nice place, perhaps not as big as the old Hyatt or Shangri-La or Cinnamon Grand further up the way she'd come, but even now, stripped of almost everything of value, overgrown with weeds and surrounded by garbage on three sides, it held some small feeling of luxury. Nobody else lived here. She climbed the rusted hulks of Mercedes-Benz cars piled up almost to the first floor and sat on her balcony.

The box had little: a few packets of fuel biscuits, salt, water. Less than what she'd had last time. Much less than what they'd given her the time before that.

'The Bluetooth device is ready to pair,' shouted a familiar voice, and the oppressive silence was split by violins and twirling flutes. A man and a woman sang about their love for each other.

She had no one to sing to or with; alone in her castle of glass, steel and garbage, she clutched her spear and listened to the voices. Presently she fell asleep again.

12:00 p.m. Monday, said the Radio. Yet another Monday.

≈

The Pissa arrived three Mondays later.

She was never quite sure how he found her. One day there was a loud clang outside her window. She picked up the spear, moving with speed borne of practiced terror, and peered outside to see a boy bouncing down the cars. She saw just enough of his face to see a look of great surprise painted on it, the mouth opened in a comically wide and silent scream. Seconds later, he hit the ground hard and went 'Ooof!'

She winced in sympathy, but tightened her grip on her spear.

The fall, however, seemed to have done nothing to the boy. He picked himself up, spat out the dust, sniffed a little, and began his climb up to her again.

Her spear landed beside him with a sharp screech, burying itself in the rusted metal of a car. It quivered a little. She watched from the darkness as he leaped back, his eyes tracking the trajectory. He put up his hands and backed away very slowly.

She breathed.

But that night, the spear thudded back into her window, making her leap and screech soundlessly with shock.

She crawled to the window again and looked down. It was him. Waving and laughing and leaping in the moonlight, like the lunatic that he clearly must be. It was then that she realized that tied to the end of the spear was a packet of biscuits and a blue badge with a 1 on it.

A 1! She had never seen a 1 before. She reached out and touched the badge. It was real. Her hand slid to the spear shaft.

She was still examining the badge when the boy climbed up, successfully this time, and poked his head in through the window. Reacting instinctively, she hit him on the head with the spear. Hard.

The boy slid down, unconscious. She leaped from the window and surveyed her catch.

He was tall and gangly. Unusually long limbs poked out of a gray T-shirt and shorts. There was something shiny on his wrist, like a metal band. Jewellery, perhaps. There was something odd about him; it took her a moment to realize that the boy had none of the scratches and bleeds and torn skin that she saw on every other kid she met. His skin was whole – dirty, but whole – a beautiful, uniformly textured brown.

She climbed out and crouched beside him, checking his pockets. The shorts, baggy with many pockets, were full. She emptied them. There was some ration, and a knife that folded in on itself. She played with it, entranced, until it flipped down and bit her sharply on the thumb. She hissed in pain and threw the thing away.

She pulled out the badge and put it on him, blue against gray, and stared at it for a moment. Then, shaking her head in disbelief, she ran a rolled-up blanket under his armpits and started pulling him up onto the balcony.

He woke up in the middle of the process and screamed, but she poked him a couple of times with the blunt end of the spear and he quieted down again. She hauled him inside and sat there in the darkness, trembling, spear pointed at his heart, ready to fling her tiny weight behind it and skewer him to death.

≈

When the boy woke up again, the spear-tip was hovering inches from his face.

He yelled and hauled himself up, moving backwards and taking a look at the person holding the shiny pointy thing at him.

It was the girl he had seen at the window. Dark, greasy, matted wires for hair, hanging down in filthy locks. One arm made thick for warding off knives, wrapped with black cloth. Filthy clawed feet that gripped the broken concrete with ease.

The eyes scared him a little.

'Epa!' he blurted, hands up. 'Don't!'

Eyes flicked to his hands, then back to him. She tossed him something.

It was his badge, blue with the neat 1 on it.

'Yes, I'm from 1,' he said. He reached into his pockets to pull out a biscuit, perhaps offer one to her in peace.

His pockets were empty.

She watched him curiously, then put the spear down and disappeared. She reappeared with a tin cup of hot water and one of his biscuit packets. Deftly, she slit it open with her spear. The black, crumbly thing fell into the water and made thin, dark soup. She pushed it at him with the spear.

He blew on it and drank half, then pushed the cup back towards her.

That seemed to ease things a little. The spear was taken away. She pulled out a silver box – a radio, one of those old steel solar types. There was a cassette inside. She fiddled a bit with it and pressed a button.

'Who are you?' said the Radio in a toneless male voice. A button press. 'We must find food.' A frown. More fiddling. More button pressed. 'Where are you from?'

Ah. Now he understood her silence.

He told her the truth. He told her he was from Colombo 1, where the lightbulbs worked and there was electricity in the walls and the trains shuddered and screamed at night. He told her he had run away.

She pointed out of the window with the spear. The Mountain was clearly visible.

'Yes. Colombo 1. Other side,' he said slowly, miming.

She seemed to have trouble with the concept.

He tried miming again. I-ran-away-over-the-Mountain. He held his nose, waved. Stinky-mountain.

She looked at him inscrutably.

Can-I-stay-here.

She shook her head.

'I need a place to stay,' he said.

She pointed with the spear and mimed back. Out-there.

'I can't,' he protested. 'I promise I won't harm you. I just need to sleep. I just need somewhere to sleep. You can have my food!'

You-have-my-food. Dark-outside. Can't-see. Just-sleep.

And there were things out there in the darkness. He thought they were children, but if they were, they made her look tame.

She stared at him again, then nodded, the slightest of nods.

That night, she watched him sleep.

≈

And thus began their strange friendship. One night turned into two; two turned into three. Three turned into the Pissa foraging, coming back with water, cloth, old packets of biscuits, all sorts of scraps, and her warily accepting them, swift fingers discarding the spoiled, the rotten. And that turned into four days. Before long, another Monday was there.

He was a thin boy, but built tall, all elbows and knees and curiosity. He had no sense for what was good and bad; she knew he would die out there without her.

Slowly she taught him her ways. How to find the sea. How to be silent, to keep in the shadows and move quietly, and to know never to get boxed in.

She showed him the US Embassy, and the gun turrets, and the President's House, and how to run between them without getting shot. Once he got too close to the guns and they whirred and spat out one bullet. It hit nothing, but it was like thunder. From then on he leaned to move warily, low and fast.

She took him through the corpses of the Colombo hotels, their underbellies stuffed with rusted hulks of cars, their foyers and lounges offering discounts to customers that had died long before the two of them had even existed.

She showed him the Sons of Cinnamon, showed him what enough children could do to someone, if they had knives and weren't afraid to fight like dogs. She showed him the Swimming Clubbers, who were said to bathe in the sea from time to time, despite the salt water being bad for their bodies.

Then there were the Shangri-Las, the One People, who swam in their pools and hung the corpses of those who trespassed from tubes of purple neon. Once these wars had been fought with accountants and hostile takeovers and political ties and family connections. Now they were fought with spear and knife in the shade of the mountain of garbage.

He was brave, she would give him that. Not the fastest in the heart or the head, but he foraged far and wide, and broke her old routines.

Like ghosts, the two children slid in and out of the places built to keep people out, clanking gently. They passed through places once built to hold in the beauty of Colombo – glass cubes that had once come with slick waiters and exorbitant prices. They trod in the shadow of the new rich and the powerful – the children who could summon armies, who held entire tribes in thrall, shouting from thrones built out of dead vehicles.

Finally, she took him down to the Line on Monday.

The other kids left him alone, mostly because he was ... strange. Something about him made even the fiercest of them pause. Perhaps it was his unbroken skin and his long limbs, or perhaps it was the way he always looked them straight in the eyes.

Two of them tried. They must have been from Ramada, or maybe even from Galle Face Hotel, because they were built big. They pushed him down. But he could fight; he knocked one down, grabbed the bat he held, and swung at the other. There was a loud crack, a blaring scream and the sound of angry sobbing.

As she watched, someone appeared at her side. He was thin and rakish, with protruding eyes.

'Silent girl tribe?' he said with a voice like gravel, pointing towards the Pissa.

She shook her head.

'You know rules,' said the gravel-child quietly. 'Tribe?'

She did know the rules. Hesitantly, she nodded.

'You will tell when tribes meet?'

Oh well. She nodded again.

The gravel-child whistled and disappeared. The bullies backed off. The Pissa was officially in her tribe now. She was responsible for him, and in return they would do him no harm.

She sighed and waved at him. Come-come-come.

At the next tribe meeting, she pointed to Pissa, then to herself, then to the Radio. Pissa-her-Radio.

My-people-us.

And so they let Pissa be, even when he walked on Galle Face with no weapons; even when he found that cache of alcohol at the Ministry of Defense and set it on fire, hooting gleefully. The girl just watched him in silence and, when the smoke drifted their way, held out his plastic cloak, the one with the little pockets sewn in the sides. Together they waited with the until the fire had danced itself out, the hot smoke temporarily driving out the stink of garbage.

Then she shook her head and went back to the dreary gray world she knew and lived in. He was tribe now, and that meant she was responsible.

≈

'We need food,' she blared at him with the Radio.

'I know.' Food was how he had found the cache of alcohol in the first place: there had been rumors of caches of fuel biscuits that appeared there regularly. 'We should look in Colombo 4.'

...Vigorous shaking of the head...

...DANGER.

The Mondays came and went, one after the other.

≈

He disobeyed her, of course. The girl cared for nothing but her own apartment and her room and her window and her food from the Monday Line. It all seemed terribly boring. There was little to do here other than trying to keep from getting shot, stabbed or bit.

First he went down Galle Road. He had seen the maps on the walls of the train station back home: this way led to Colombo 4. There was a sort of nameless hulk in the distance. Silence fell and grew as he walked, until only his footsteps rang out in the heat. Presently he came to a pile-up of cars, blackened and rusted.

They looked like they had been hit really, really hard.

The nameless hulk, which had gotten larger, moved, and he saw rows and rows of gun turrets. He swallowed and ran away quickly. It did not follow. He sat and thought a bit. The boy he had met from 4 – the one with the black cap – had told him the Thing could not see above it, that there was a way over the rooftops, but he had never met Black Cap again.

That left 5. 5 was ... He wavered. Ah yes. That way.

He had been walking for a while when six spears, wood tipped with knives, shuddered down around him. They were fringed with colorful streamers tied at the back. They had been dropped from above.

He shaded his eyes and backed away slowly.

When he got back, the girl was standing in the room, counting. One look and he knew. They were running out of food. Those Port City bastards were giving less and less and less. She looked at him, and he saw in her eyes a kind of mute resignation that made him want to curl up and die.

And so he told her of the one place he knew they had food. He had told himself he would never go back there, but

Colombo 1

Had

Food.

Dammit.

She thought about it. He knew when she was thinking. She hugged the radio and the spear and looked out of the window.

≈

'I met another 4-er today,' he said one evening, taping a can to something. 'Did you know they have more supply people there? Like ours, but more biscuits?'

She shook her head. Can't-get-past, she mimed. I-tried.

'They say there's plenty of stuff to see in Colombo 5 and 7,' he said, hunched over. 'Maybe even some green. They said there used to be parks where lots of green grew. Shall we go look?'

She shook her head again and made the sign for Traps and Death. She, too, had heard the stories, and she hadn't believed them until she made the run herself, back when she had others to share her world with. Four of them had gone in, and only she had made it back.

'Look!' he cried happily, holding out the can he'd been working on. As far as she could see, he had made some holes at the bottom and taped it over with cloth.

'Look,' he repeated, dipping it into the water and holding it, cloth side down, over a white porcelain plate.

It took a while for her to realize that the water coming out of the can was clear. No mud. No muck. She admired it and he grinned. 'Let's see what we got today.'

She pulled out the box of rations and they looked at it.

'There isn't much,' he said at last.

She agreed. This time there was barely enough for one person. She reached for the Radio and fumbled through the cassettes and pressed a button.

'We need food,' the Radio said.

She looked around. They were on the rooftop of their hotel; and from here, the setting sun carved pink and gold into the sky, painting even the polluted hell of Colombo with a soft kind of beauty. In the distance, the sea rose to meet the sky, pulling it down, drawing a flat line across the world. The Pissa read her thoughts, like he always did.

'It's beautiful,' he said.

She pressed the button on the Radio again. 'We need food,' it repeated, with none of the sadness that she felt inside.

TWO

They set out a couple of Mondays later, clanking gently across cracked pavements.

Had there been anyone left to tell them of it, the two children could have heard a long and fantastic tale as they walked, a tale of Colombo and the little island they lived on. They could have been told about the children of Bambalapitiya, or Colombo 4, a thick jungle where bandits would once hide and waylay goods shuttled Colombo and between Galle, a city in the South. The two children would have then pointed out the irony in this, because today, many thousands of years later, Colombo 4 was still just that; a den of bandits and thieves.

They could have learned of the Portuguese invading Colombo in the 1600s, building the fort that later became known as Colombo Fort – or Colombo 1, the heart of Colombo. They could have learned of Colombo 3, or Kollupitiya, which got its name when rich and powerful

Ceylonese ousted others from their lands, and began to call it Kolla-ke-pitiya, 'Stolen land'.

And had the two children been capable of such thought, they would have pointed out the curious, cyclical nature of history, for today, in this land of filth, Colombo 3 was still a stolen land; stolen by the Portuguese, the British, the Chinese, and now by themselves.

But there was no one left to tell this tale, and so the two small figures passed under the watchful eyes of lookouts and automated missile defenses alike – soft-footed, cautious children, taking what they could. At midnight they were challenged – it was the turn of the Children of the Taj to guard Galle Face.

'Silent girl is crazy.' said the leader of the crew, an urchin – awkward, angry.

Silent girl shrugged. It was, the Pissa had to admit, a very eloquent shrug.

'Nobody comes back from the Blue Mountain.'

She shrugged again and nodded to the Pissa. The unwritten Law said they had to pay tribute. From the bag he pulled out two packets of biscuits and a steel-thing – which people had once called a Macbook – thrown in to sweeten the deal. The leader sharpened his knife on the edge of the steel-thing while his men opened the beans.

'Why?' asked the leader. 'Why go there?'

The Pissa backed up her inevitable shrug with a stony stare. The leader tried to stare him down, but something about them spooked him. He gestured – and they were let through.

The girl peered at the stinking hill that rose in front of them, vomiting itself all over the towers of the city. In the darkness it was too large, too vast, like a curtain between the earth and the sky. A single great mountain of garbage, long since collapsed, polythene and filth baked in the sun to a hard consistency. A stinking fluid sloshed out from it – leachate, water condensed from the filth.

She mimed. You – came – over – this?

'It's not as bad as it smells,' he lied.

She made to light a torch, but he grabbed her hand.

'No fire,' he said urgently. 'It burns.'

Mystified, she obeyed him.

Well, there was nothing to it. 'Come with me,' he said, scrawny arms hoisting himself up onto the mountain of trash. 'There's a way through here.'

If she ever remembered of those first few hours, it was only as one long, squelching nightmare – a nightmare that grew steadily easier as they climbed. The smell of rotten eggs enveloped them. From time to time the Pissa stumbled, and she pulled him back. The sense of adventure faded; all that was left was the grim determination of children.

They climbed. First two stories, then five, then ten, then twenty, then forty, until the slopes grew less steep and all of Colombo lay stretched out before their eyes. But it was night now; all there was to see was darkness. Presently the Pissa found them a cave. Perhaps it had been natural once, but now it was propped up here and there with plastic pipes, umbrella rods and steel beams. The polythene, beaten by the sun and the wind, was quite dry underneath; the ground felt more like rubber than anything else.

She sat down, exhausted and stinking, and they shared a drink of water. She turned to him. How-much-further?

'Just a little bit,' he said. They sat there in silence, watching the moonlight play with the city they were leaving behind. The great glass dome that covered the Port City gleamed and flashed.

The Pissa was hungry. 'That's where they keep the food, isn't it?' he said.

She thought about it and reached for her cassettes. She slid one into the Radio with great care and hit the button.

'Welcome to the Colombo Port City,' the Radio said crisply, in more dulcet tones than usual. 'A paradise crafted by the greatest engineers this world has ever seen. Living spaces, office buildings, recreational facilities, a full, artificial weather system – our state of the art biodome will keep you and yours safe for as long as you stay here. For inquiries and reservations call 011 88 77 66 55 44 22 3. Free yourself. Come join us at the Colombo Port City. Limited slots available – apply now!'

The Pissa eyed the Radio curiously and then looked at her.

'Where did you get that?' he asked.

From-a-friend. Friend-dead, she mimed.

'Can I see it?'

She shook her head, but did not stop him when he reached out and gingerly took a cassette in his hands. She loaded another one and hit play.

'Reading Storagecraft dot com,' said the Radio, a little less crisply, in a more muted voice. 'The sad truth about data storage is that no medium for data storage will last forever. Most of them are replaced by a new storage method before long. But just how long will your favourite storage method last? According to the US National Archives, CDs and

DVDs have very similar lifespans. Generally, unrecorded CDs and DVDs have a shelf-life of five to ten years. The life expectancy of recorded CDs and DVDs is between two and five years, though based on manufacturer claims, ten to twenty five years, or even longer, isn't unprecedented. Most hard disk drives (HDD) last between three and five years before some component fails. eHow says flash drives can last up to ten years. Magnetic tape, such as cassette tape, can realistically last about ten to twenty years.'

'What is ... toragecraft?'

She shrugged.

'Dot? Com?'

She shrugged again. All she knew was that this cassette spoke about cassettes.

The Pissa handed back the device reverently, and curled up and went to sleep.

≈

When dawn finally arrived, it was the most spectacularly thing she had ever seen in her life.

First there was a lightness, a sort of soft gray half-light like that first cough, like that hesitant drumbeat. The blue-black of the night receded, prowling around this new thing that had appeared. Then, the Sun appeared: a half-disc, glowing, the lone trumpet, pitching in, signaling the rest of the orchestra to begin. And then the gold exploded everywhere, flinging its arms and dispelling the night. Cloud swirled in glee. She gasped. It was just so beautiful.

Dawn revealed what the night had not: the city-Colombo, Galle Face – far, far below them, cut off from them by the waterway. And around them the skeletons of steel and glass towers, some of them half-buried in the filth, signs poking out from the mountain of trash. Hilton, said one.

She turned; in front of her rose the mountain of garbage, stretching into the sky. She could make out a tip, and a sort of track leading to it. Someone had planted a flag just up ahead – a large T-shirt, actually. *Sinha-Le*, it said, flapping proudly on top of a mountain of trash.

'THE BLUETOOTH DEVICE HAS CONNECTED SUCCESSFULLY,' said a voice from far below them. It was much quieter now. A broodingly beautiful whine cut through, overlaid with a what to her sounded like people screaming in perfect harmony. She shuddered, not knowing that once people had paid to hear the ghoulish sounds of Mozart's Lacrimosa Requiem.

The Pissa woke up with the music, and went to scout out ahead. She watched his angular frame inch away, and then return.

'We need to take a left in a little bit,' he decided. 'There's a road that goes down from here, just around the corner. You know where the canal is on the other side?

No, she did not.

'Well, it ends there,' he said. 'The old maps said there's something called Dutch Hospital under us. A hospital! Under this! Can you imagine?'

His stomach whined. She gave him his share of the biscuits – almost their last packet. Is-there-food? She mimed.

He seemed to hesitate.

'There is food,' he said at last. 'There's a lot of things in Colombo 1.'

She didn't like the way he hesitated. Well, she reasoned. If it didn't work, if there really was no end to the Mountain, like some believed, at least she knew the way back.

They climbed. The wind, stirring occasionally, blew scraps of paper in her face. Old, yellowed newspapers.

'British quell American uprising,' said one.

'Marxist rebellion destroyed, Queen declares Kandy new seat of governance,' read another.

They made no sense to her. She pushed them aside and kept climbing, spear clutched tight.

THREE

Two days later, two children crested a gigantic mountain of rubbish.

They were gaunt and filthy; their skins flaked and shriveled; their arms and knees blackened with the filth they stood on. They teetered briefly on the edge, puppets pushed on by the morning breeze, lit up by the rising sun.

One of them pointed and gestured. 'See? Down! Down!'

The other just stood there, her parched mouth open in a rictus of wonder and fear. She stared because she could not believe the sight that shimmered many hundreds of feet below her. It was a city: a network of wide roads crested on both sides by buildings that ranged from the flat and quintessentially boxy Ceylonese to the proud, column-flanked colonial architecture. To the left was sprawling white palace lit by ghastly blue light; it was topped with iron gates and sprinkled with cruel-looking bits of metal. A giant hand erupted like a fist from the earth, clutching what was once called a telephone. To the right was a riot of shelves and color, and beyond it a gleaming canal, topped by a metal bridge that curved over it with a strange sinuousness, like a snake.

And the people.

The people.

They were all in gray, these people; the kind of gray that is just dark enough to not be white, yet white enough to dirty easily. They moved, but not in the disordered, pack-like clusters of Colombo; here they moved in neat streams along pavements, stopping every so often at the market. They paired; they disconnected; they moved on; they switched up; they crossed streets in orderly waves; every so often they stopped, to buy, or perhaps to sell, or just to talk. And no one screamed, no one was stabbed, no one fell.

She tried to say something, but her lips only moved in silence. The Pissa crawled up next to her and started to point.

'That's the gate,' he said.

She saw, down below, the thing to which he pointed. A cracked, black road ran from under the Mountain and to a thing of metal slabs slammed into the road. There were gaps in it, small enough for a child to sneak through – or for a child to stay and spear someone through. It stretched from a tall, grimy white building to the blackened and murky waters of a canal that slurped silently through this new place.

She followed his finger to the glint of metal tracks, upwards. 'Railroad – Train Station,' he said. Long, thin roads, more metal than tarmac, radiated from it in all directions: the biggest of them snaked behind the market, and into longer distances, weaving cautiously behind buildings. The finger jumped at the buildings on either side of the gate. 'Guns. Snipers.'

The turrets made sense now. She signed. We-go-in?

He shook his head and pointed to the buildings on the other side of the canal; a line of blackened and blasted rooftops and a road sandwiched between the canal and the lake. He mimed them moving around the Gate, past the canal, past the blackened buildings. 'Halfway House,' he said. 'Safe passage.'

This-home?

He shook his head. 'I come from the other side. Around the Gate and to a set of buildings by the lake. Other side of lake?'

He took out his badge, the one with the nicely lettered '1' on it, flipped it, and pressed down. A red light started pulsing from the badge.

'They sent me into 1 as a spy,' he explained. 'Things went wrong. Had to make a run for it. Ended up on your side. You ready? They'll know we're coming now. The Halfway House will be open.'

Mystified, she nodded.

'This way,' said the boy, leading her down.

The closer she got, the less the sun beat on her, and the more she could see of the people. Some of them were larger than the others by half. Adults, perhaps, like the ones from the Monday Line at the Port City, but without the power armor.

She began to see patterns. It was clear the Adults ran the place. They pointed and whistled and waved, and children crossed streets and moved lines in direct obedience. Every so often one of the Adults would come and talk to another Adult, and they would forget everything else and talk; but when a child came to talk to them they were waved away with a frown.

She caught the boy's shoulder and pointed, and made the sign for What-is-that.

'Adults,' he said.

What-for?

He thought a bit. 'Same as Adults back there,' he said at last, pointing back over the Mountain. 'They decide who gets to eat.'

He pointed to what she had thought were broken bits of buildings hanging off the roof nearest to them. But they were cages, and inside them were children. They looked like they had been stripped bare of all skin. Wires and metal poked at unnatural angles from their bodies.

'That's what happens if the Adults see us,' he said. He explained, haltingly, in terms she could understand. His hand encompassed all of Colombo 1. Like the Sons of Cinnamon, he said, but larger, much larger, more dangerous.

Never get caught.

She thought about this as they trudged down. With each step she took, Colombo 1 grew closer and closer, and she clutched her spear tighter, heading into an uncertain world.

Presently night fell, and with it the sound of people ceased. The stars came out in the sky.

Eventually there was no more down to go. They had come to a great rusted barrier of Steel exactly like the one that they had seen not three days ago. It stood in front of the cracked road and the Gate, as if to hold back the Mountain.

A white light, like the ones from the US Embassy, flashed and carved a path between them and the Gate, lighting up the shattered expanse and moving on.

'Stay down!' hissed the boy. 'Don't let them see you.'

She crouched in the garbage, terrifyingly aware of all the gray people just ahead, even though she couldn't see them now past the bulk of the Gate. One hand held on tight to the sharpened stick. Over here the garbage had a different smell, drier and dustier, like something left too long in the closet. There they waited for a while, and at a signal from the Pissa, they moved again in the darkness.

The buildings glinted white in the moonlight, lit up by the pale blue-white beams that arced and leaped across the roads. From down here, everything looked so much bigger. The blasted hulks they were supposed to be heading for came into view.

They moved among the perimeter of the garbage until Pissa found what he was looking for: a hole big enough for them to slide through. Suddenly the barrier was gone, and all that stood between them and the Gate and safety was a stretch of floodlit road.

'This is the hard part,' he whispered, tense.

She held him back. They had to avoid the light. There was a pattern to how the beams splayed over the road. She didn't know much about this part of the world, but she knew lights and how to avoid them. If she watched long enough...

Ah, there it was. She pointed. See? See? Here-here-here-there. She had trained the Pissa enough. He should see it too.

He nodded, and they sprinted across the road, lithe bodies deftly dancing in the darkness between the beams. Here they stepped back, and here forward, until eventually, they came to the road that led straight down, the road between the lake and the canal, and the beams were held back by the shadow of the decrepit buildings.

He pointed to a mass of large buildings on the right; the Halfway House. She gaped at the buildings, at how clean they looked, but he pulled at her with the new urgency, and they moved on, along a darkened street that went down, down and down. For here was something she had not seen from up above; a thin barrier that ran from one end of the street to the other, barbed wire and barrels.

Left and right, right and left they ducked, until they had rolled beneath a large old fashioned roller gate and came to a halt in the silence.

'There are people here, too,' he whispered in the darkness.

And she felt the boy leave her. She would have panicked, but she had no words to panic with. All she could do was sit there in the darkness with the makeshift wooden spear clutched tightly in her hand.

She couldn't remember how long it was, but eventually she felt his hand on her shoulder again. 'Put this on,' he said. 'Snipers won't shoot gray. Hurry.'

In the half light she could see him getting dressed. She did as he did. A damp cloth appear from nowhere, wiping her face, her arms, her legs. She beat it away. The boy grinned – she could see his teeth curve – and tossed it to her, miming for her to repeat. She did it, not knowing why or how.

They waited.

FOUR

At dawn, two thin, silent children in gray crept out of the abandoned warehouse by the old police checkpoint. Buildings loomed beside faint yellow streetlamps.

It was into one of these that they trotted, pausing every so often to look back over their shoulders.

She was hungry, the last of the fuel biscuits gone. Her long, filthy wire-locks were tied back unsuccessfully with a twisted polythene shopping bag – a garish thing of green and pink – and looked completely out of place. She was also confused: the old familiar landmarks were gone, and this skyline was new; it was disorienting, and that made her angry. She glared at the coming sun with animal-like intensity, her fear making her angry.

'We'll take the side streets,' he said confidently. He was at home here; tall, his wrists poking out of his sleeves, eyes darting from a face that had been scrubbed almost raw. 'We can get to the Halfway House. We can find some food...'

'Halt!' said a voice like thunder.

They froze. Her wolf-face vanished and was replaced by pure terror.

Two strong arms gripped them and swiveled them around.

'The smell!' shouted the thunder-voice. 'Which division are you two from? Eh?'

The boy stood up straighter and puffed out his chest and shouted back a string of numbers.

Thunder-voice sniffed. 'That batch, eh? And where are you going? And why the hell does this one smell so bad? Eh?' This one was addressed more to the girl than the boy.

She responded the only way she knew. In one fluid motion she leaped forward and thrust the stick into the groin. Thunder-voice doubled up with an 'Oof!' And she kicked him in the head.

A child would have blacked out, but Adults without their armor were squishier; there was a crunch, and her foot came away wet and slick.

'Run!' said the boy, pulling her away.

And they ran. Arms flailing, legs going thump-thump thump on pavements, they ran down the street, the buildings and the color and the noise growing nearer with each thudding step. People jumped aside as they passed. She flew past gray bodies. They stared at her, eyes open with alarm and interest; she, accustomed to the brutal streets of Colombo 3, saw only snarls and danger.

Finally, they found themselves in a long, lonely tunnel.

'Never,' he whispered, trembling and panting. 'Never do that again.'

She nodded, taking stock of where they were. The tunnel was about two, maybe three stories high; stairs ran down from it to roads that alternated between concrete and metal. The same kind of metal she had seen at the bridge back there, actually. There was a stench in the air – something hot, something electric.

The confusion intensified. She spun around, eyes darting for familiarity, and found none. She ran a hand over the bag still tied to her shoulder. Radio – tins – food packets. She pulled out the Radio because she was bursting with questions, but he hurriedly pushed it back inside.

'It's not safe,' he whispered. 'Not until we get to the Halfway House.'

They began walking again, only this time much more slowly; heads bent, bags slung over their shoulders, gray figures moving through the empty, cavernous checkpoint. The presence of people made her nervous. Every so often she would dart behind a pillar, or a sign, and pull at the boy; he would just shake his head and motion her, urgently, onwards.

He took her through the back gate, where weeds and vines grew on a solid green wall that could be climbed without difficulty, and across the broken road behind it, and then to the nest of buildings behind that. They had crumbled on themselves. The most open had a sign outside, rusted, that said '*Baileys Casino*'.

He pointed at it, then mimed going through, and skirting the lake on the other side.

She nodded. I-slow, she mimed. She could feel the exhaustion coming on. She had given him the last biscuit.

Her stomach whined.

He nodded, and they ran for it.

A high roof. A turnstile. She leaped over it. Someone shouted. A staircase. The Pissa outpaced her flagging steps. Up, up, up and up. And then – a little ahead of her the Pissa skidded and vaulted nimbly over a turnstile. She followed without thinking.

'Messenger, Class 3,' the Pissa was saying to the Adult halfway up the stairs. 'I'm taking the rookie on a training run. She messed up a bit, fell in the canal. You know how the first run is.'

This Adult was a girl. She had long hair and her face was as large as the Silent girl's arm, and she sat in a pool of darkness with only one yellow light to keep her company. Silent girl brought up her stick.

'Walking stick,' said the boy unnecessarily. The Adult waved them on. As they passed, the Adult gave her a sort of wink and a thumbs-up. She clutched her stick, mystified, and hurried up. Soon, she was spat out on the other side; a mere strip of road lay between them and the vast cavern of the Halfway House. They rushed in, fleeing the shouting that was becoming more insistent now.

'Come on,' he said, taking her hand, and they plunged ever inward, picking their way around and over the ruins of the casino that had once stood here. The years had stripped away the light and the merry colors; all that was left was a graveyard of tables half-rotted to the ground, and gold flaked paint that peeled slowly off fungus-laden walls.

There were holes in the walls, arches that lined up. He took her through one building after another, slowly following the curve of the river, two ghosts flitting from the cover of ruins and over metal gates. The unrelenting blackness of the lake curled to their right. To their left they could see the curve of buildings that they had fled from; as the sun rose higher, they fled deeper and deeper into whatever cover they could find, acutely aware of how visible they were.

They were not alone. Children lurked here, dressed in gray, but unlike the orderly children of the roads, these were wild. They peered at the two newcomers from dark corners. The girl could feel them following. It was the crunch and whine of motors in the darkness; the way hands wreathed in rust reached out of the dark corners to grip on half-rotted columns in the buildings they crashed through.

'We come in peace,' said the Pissa. He held up his hands. Empty. Palms out. 'We come in peace! We travel through and do not see you.'

The darkness paused, lingering.

'We do not see you,' the Pissa repeated softly.

The darkness went away with a crunch of footsteps.

The two travellers turned their tired steps forward again and plodded onwards. They were flagging, now, and Silent girl could no longer see properly; there were too many shadows, and every so often she crashed into something with a crack and a loud thunk. Her skin felt burning hot to the touch. They had never run this far without rest, without water, without biscuits...

And no orientation. She was getting a sense of it, now; the water on the right side, the sun there – but it was strange and unfamiliar and confusing.

Presently they came to a place that was closed, unlike all the others; maybe they were tired and slow, for they had not had anything to eat in a while, but here there were no holes, only a cavernous emptiness with stairs lit in dim gloom.

Suddenly a voice rang out, clear and bright.

'What is this tree?'

The Pissa ran forward.

'What is this tree?' the voice demanded.

'It's a mango tree!' said the Pissa hoarsely.

'Are there mango trees other than this one?'

'Yes!' shouted the Pissa into the darkness. 'Yes, many!'

'Besides this mango tree and other mango trees, are there other trees?'

'Yes! There are other trees besides this tree and other mango trees!'

'Besides those trees and other mango trees, are there any other trees?'

'There's this mango tree!' said the Pissa triumphantly. 'It's me! It's me!'

The voice laughed, echoing. The Pissa laughed, too. It was the most beautiful thing the Silent girl had ever heard.

There was the sound of bolts snapping back in their locks and the greasy crunch of oiled gates sliding.

'Welcome to the Halfway House,' said the voice.

Hungry and exhausted beyond all endurance, Silent girl slumped forward, the spear falling from her hands with a clatter.

FIVE

The Pissa told her, much later, that she had been unconscious for almost everything that followed right after. The world passed by in fragments she remembered; darkness and light, darkness and light, flickering in and out. There was a girl with a burnt face. She looked pale, almost dead, like something that had never seen the sun. She hissed, or perhaps she spoke, but the voice came from the far edge of exhaustion where sound didn't work like it normally did. The Silent girl remembered a tunnel, and splashing, and then a great, wet silence, a rocking motion, and stars floating above, mirrored in the black waters that bore them away from the gray people and the ruins of the Halfway House.

And then there was another boy, a strange one with many binoculars strung around his neck and many watches strapped to his wrist. He was opening her up. He held two wires in one hand, and they sparked, and her mouth opened in the soundless 'O' of a scream when they touched her.

'You're awake!' the Pissa said, over and over.

And then there was an Adult, waiting for them at the moonlit edge of the boundary where the water ended. He was thin and very tall, taller than anyone she'd ever seen, and wore some kind of black armor. He had huge hands and long hair of a strange color, gray mixed in with the usual black. He was flanked by two boys, and seemed very surprised to see them.

Hands clamped on her. She twisted one and broke the other before things went dark again.

'It's safe, it's safe!' said the Pissa's voice, far away. Then, in a lower voice: 'Kanishkersir, battery one. She's not eating.'

Hands picked her up then. Large hands, Adult hands. She tried to swat them away, but they were surprisingly strong: they forced her mouth open, put something in, closed it, turned her head this way and that. She kicked and protested and bit.

'This should help,' said the Adult. He had a voice like gravel. He said, 'you need to tell me what the hell happened.'

They moved noiselessly through the night, her limp body still carried by the Adult. The Pissa started to talk. She thought he was apologizing to the Adult, at first, but then he was telling a story, a story about a place on the other side of a mountain of trash, where there was a girl who lived alone in a tower, like a queen.

They put her in a box, and let her be.

≈

She came to herself in a gray daze. The only thing she could focus on was a red glare of familiar numbers in front of her.

'2.30 A.M., MONDAY', read the Radio.

But it stayed silent. She waiting for that awful voice to scream its nonsense about Bluetooth, but there was nothing but silence.

Slowly her eyes focussed, and she began to see where she was. It was some sort of room, but large, like one of the halls that the Children of Cinnamon lived in. But here, instead of carpet and rotted paint and fungus-covered curtains was brick, unadorned. One side was glass-fronted, but the moonlight ended before her feet began; she could look without being seen. She remembered the Adult and the strength of those arms with a shudder, and tried to move.

Something whined and protested inside her.

She knew that whine. That was when she ran out of water, and couldn't move her feet; sometimes she had to crawl to where she kept the bottles. She tried, but this was not her apartment, and she hit a wall. The gray daze came over her again, and she drifted into sleep.

She woke up again when the door creaked open, and a shape moved in. She tried to scream, but the shape resolved itself into the Pissa.

He opened his arms – there was food there, and water in bottles. She dropped her spear.

'It's safe here,' he said gently, as she retreated into the darkness, feet dragging uselessly behind her, clutching a water bottle. 'You don't need to worry. We'll keep you safe.'

That night she slept in the darkness again, with him curled up outside, a spear in his hand in case anything happened.

SIX

A week later, the Pissa sat with the Silent girl on on the pavement outside her little brick-box-hall.

It was a few days after that strange first night, and cautious but curious, she had come out of the hall where she slept to explore the rest of this strange new world.

The Pissa had told her they were some way away from Colombo 1, in a safe place: where exactly it was she could not tell, for it was ringed around with high brick walls. Her hall – which she now thought of as her house – was one of rows of hundreds of other houses, all exactly alike. There was a road that ran between them and looped in on itself; these, and the sky, were her only view.

A group of children ran past, their footsteps hitting the ground in perfect unison. Left-right-left-right, every second, like a clock with many arms and legs.

'That's Time,' the Pissa said, pointing to the boy with many watches as he ran, dragging his feet a little, at the back of this strange formation. 'His real name is Twenty Three, but we all call him Time. He's the one who fixed you up on the raft.'

She remembered. Or rather, she had a vague memory of it; of him holding cables that sparked and shuddered with electricity.

'That's Fourteen, he's just a little bit younger than me, and Nineteen,' the Pissa continued, 'and Burnt girl you've already met. She guards the tunnel for us. You know they tried to burn this place down? That's when her face melted.'

She let him chatter on, filing what he said away for later. For now, she needed to find out what all these people were doing here. The 'they' were the gray people. Who was 'us'?

At least there was food here. Three packets of biscuits a day for each child – a luxury. And plenty of places to walk where nobody would stab you or garotte you and try to take your food away.

She ate a biscuit as she pondered this, feeling the fuel hit her body.

'So what do you think?' the Pissa asked.

She searched for cassettes, found the one that said, 'Good,' and played it at him. He smiled.

A sharp clap broke the evening silence. The running children halted. It was the Adult, the one with strange hair. The one the Pissa called Kanishkersir. He clapped again at them, and made a rotating gesture. Other side now. Other side.

The children turned around and began the run the other way. They ran past the two sitting children, calling out to the Pissa as they went by. He grinned, and joined them on the next circuit, laughing with the others, one child among many running through an old office complex under the dry Colombo sun.

'What is this tree?' one of them chanted, his voice thin and piercing.

'It is a mango tree!' they shouted.

'Are there mango trees other than this one?'

'Yes!' shouted all the running shouted, the Pissa shouting with them. 'Yes, many!'

She stood up and reached for the new spear she had fashioned out of a tree branch, and then followed the running children at a distance, peering in into the houses as she passed. There was indoor-grass on some of the floors, and long strange rows of desks and chairs where children could sit and face one another. Wires stuck out from the walls and tables. If she had been from another time she would have been able to read the signboards, neatly preserved and meticulously scrubbed.

TRIPOLI MARKET, read one. TRAINING ZONE 1, said another in angry yellow and black. In another era, long gone by, this had been a center of bustle and trade, the chaos of vegetable sellers spilling over onto the streets that were now too orderly, neat, unstained. In another lifetime, back alleys had led to a Colombo 1 bereft of the iron gates that now barred entry, and throngs of people had walked under the hot sun from one to the other, sweating in the heat and humidity.

She knew nothing of this. All she knew was that this was not Colombo 1. Colombo 1, the promised land, was what they had run from. This was somewhere beyond. The Pissa's badge with '1' on it had been stolen, or perhaps made; he had spent some time among the gray people; there was some kind of lying there. He tried to explain the concept of a spy, but it eluded her; all she knew was he had dressed like them to feel safer.

The children ran by the outer wall, between what she now understood was Colombo 1 – and another, a darker thing walled off by long, filthy roads and high metal gates. She had tried to explore that way, but there were guards who gestured her back; children like her, dressed in faded khaki several sizes too big for them, carrying strange large things that made a dreadful roaring sound. Guns, the Pissa had told her, pointing. He pointed at the gun, pointed at himself, fell over. Point, point, fall over. Guns. Dead. Guns make dead.

She took one look at the children who held the guns, and saw flat eyes, dull eyes, the kind that didn't care if they lived or died. Children back home had had those eyes. They were killers. She understood then that these were like the automated guns of the Embassy back home, except these guns had bodies and could move.

And so she went back to the carpeting and the children who sat in chairs in straight lines and thought about the question. The Pissa had assured her that she would not miss a thing about Colombo 3: there was food here, and water.

She decided, after much deliberation, that it was a lie he believed in. She missed the tall places, the silence of the streets, the sea, even on hot days, when it stank.

But there was food here and water.

And people.

Every day she woke up with the new spear in her hand, convinced that she would wake up to find bodies broken, spears thrust through bellies, the Pissa dying in a corner. That the food and water would run out and the blood would spill, just like it had back in Colombo 3.

And every day Tripoli proved her wrong: the sun shone, the street was clean, and the children ate, ran, and did not kill each other. She expected them to break out into gangs and stone each other. They did not. Any fights that happened were broken up quickly and efficiently, the combatants send to their houses with barely a scratch on their bodies.

She could take them, if she wanted to; she knew that. They were strong and well-fed, but also stupid. They did not check the corners when they entered a room; they did not understand what it meant to strike first, and hard, and fast, and to flee before they could catch you; like idiots, they shouted at each other, and pushed each other, as if more to prove a point than to actually hurt. She did not understand how or why they lived like this, but it felt good sometimes to sit and to watch, and to not have to run.

The Adult came to her once while she watched, perched on one of the walls, just out of the range of the guards.

'Kaawada?' Ate? A familiar greeting from an unfamiliar face.

She nodded, tapping her belly. He was tall, and loomed over her, the power armor glinting gently in the sun. She watched his long gray-black hair, curious, and stretched out a tentative hand to it as it blew in the breeze. It was so unlike hers.

The Adult warily allowed her to tug on a few strands and sift them through her hands.

'Thirteen tells me you're from Colombo 3.'

Nod.

'What's your designation? What build are you?'

There was an answer to that: she knew the answer. EXPLORER-TYPE-3-BUILD-8. She pulled the Radio to her, but it had nothing that could speak the right words. She made the gesture. Can't-speak.

'How many others live in 3?'

Maybe thirty, maybe forty. She made the sign.

'Damn Ministry,' the Adult said, almost to himself. 'Alright, little one. Run diagnostics.' He recited a string of numbers. 'Send the report to that address.'

And then he walked away and went and stood on a hillock some distance away, looking at something. The shadows were a little longer.

She picked up her slippers and trotted over, moving at a confident clip. That was another strange thing they did here. Someone moving with their head high was completely ignored. Move slowly and with normal caution and they started to look.

She reached the hillock where the Adult had been standing. On the other side was the wall, a little iron gate set in it was closing.

She waited a bit, then scrabbled quickly up the wall. The brick offered plenty of handholds. She dropped on the other side, her bare feet silent on hot asphalt. Kanishkersir was just ahead, walking with his head down, between the ruins of buildings that extended past this side of the wall. His long, graying hair swung in the breeze. She followed.

He went on steadily, his rangy gait moving past rows of silent hulks of buildings, each one more rotted and mildewed than the last. And then, eventually, a road; except that it was filled from one end to another with cars, huge stacks of cars piled on top of each other, so that the road was jammed with a sea of half-crushed tires and engine parts. Here he waited.

Presently another Adult appeared from the sea of cars. He was bald and had a beard like black indoor-grass. He was dressed in white, with coarse letters on his back. MINISTRY OF RECONCILIATION, it said, though she only saw the shapes, and not the words.

'Kanishka?' this new Adult said.

'Lalith.'

Lalith-Adult held out a stick that burned and smoked on one end. Kanishkersir took it and sucked on it, puffing out smoke.

The two men puffed awhile in silence.

'So how's it on your end?'

'Doing okay,' said Kanishkersir. 'I sent one of my Connectors for the usual check on 3. Bugger stayed longer than he should have, came back with this new kid. Old model, Explorer-type. Can't talk. Fights like hell, though. Broke two wrists and almost took my arm off when we grabbed her.'

Lalith-Adult became very interested. 'I haven't seen an Explorer in years. What's happening in 3 now?'

'Not much,' said Kanishkersir. 'Bunch of really old-model kids, probably ones we've dumped. They're not aren't getting food from the Port City anymore. Looks like the Chinese have realized their little charity drive isn't working out. They say they're pulling out before the floods come in again.'

Kanishkersir nodded. They puffed in silence for a bit.

'And on your end?'

'All right. Same as last time.'

'Sea level?'

'Don't get your hopes up. The Chinese are right, there's another damned flood coming soon. Keep the boats around.'

More silence. A new stick was brought out, set on fire. The smoke drifted her way, curling lazily through the evening.

'I heard there's a war coming,' said Lalith-Adult.

This time it was Kanishkersir who was interested. 'When?'

'No idea, you know how the Ministry works, everything's last-minute,' said Lalith, his voice taking on a faint growling tone. 'Same rules. Our lot versus your lot. Livestreams, everything sent up the ladder. We get a ten percent cut this time on the betting. You have enough kids?'

'I can put up a decent defense. But I'll need new children once all this is over.'

'I hear there's a new shipment coming in from Kandy,' said Lalith-Adult. 'Maybe even few Kandyborn sent out to prove something.'

'Crazy bastards, eh?'

'It's not real to them, neh. We're not real to them.'

They puffed meditatively for a bit.

'You ever think about going home?' asked Lalith-Adult. 'Giving all of this up, taking the train back to Kandy?'

Kanishkersir shrugged. 'What am I going to do in Kandy?' he said. 'No work, no rights, I have to get on my knees every ten feet for some hill-grown prat who thinks he's gods because his grandfather's third cousin's mother was in the history books. At least the wife can walk around a bit here. Kids get to eat. Better out here than being in Kandy.'

'Hmm,' said Lalith. 'At least those buggers don't get wet.'

He dropped the burning smoke-thing to the ground and crushed it beneath his shoe. 'Well, nice seeing you again. I'll see you next week?'

'You let me know when they fix the date for the livestream.'

'Will do,' said Lalith-Adult. 'Bet you our lot kills all your kids this time. Ten thousand.'

'Ten thousand says my lot survives.'

Lalith grinned and walked back into the sea of cars. 'Ten thousand,' he said, his voice echoing faintly through the metal. 'I'll tell Accounts to cut it from your paycheck already.'

Kanishkersir, too, turned back and walked to his camp. She pressed herself into a dark crevice. He passed by so close she could smell the smelly smoke from the burning stick clinging to him. She darted out, a shadow flitting in the Adult's wake.

Kanishkersir came to the camp. He nodded to the sentries. They stood aside for him and then closed ranks again, sealing off TRIPOLI with their guns and their dead eyes.

She looked back, at where the sea of cars had been, where the Lalith-Adult had gone in. Then she looked back at TRIPOLI. And back at the sea of cars.

There was something strange here, and she needed to find out what.

Clutching her spear, she turned back to the sea of cars, and went after the Lalith.

SEVEN

It was dark, and the Pissa was getting worried.

Silent girl was wild, but she was also a creature of habit. She sometimes vanished during the day, but she was always back in their house by dark. He went to Kanishkersir, but the Adult seemed pre-occupied.

'She's probably just asleep somewhere,' he said. 'Did you do your duties today?'

'Yes sir, I did, sir.'

'The sheet has you marked for battery duty tonight.'

'Yes, sir,' said the Pissa. He hated battery duty.

Kanishkersir seemed satisfied. 'Go,' he said, flapping a hand at the Pissa. 'Oh, and Thirteen?'

He came back. 'Yes, sir?'

Kasnishkersir tapped a piece of paper on his desk. A map. The map of Colombo that the Pissa had drawn for him as soon as he had returned to the Halfway House. An almost perfect diagram of everything he'd seen from the top of the Mountain.

'I appreciate you pulling this off,' said the Adult. 'But I want you to stick to the camp now. Understand?'

'Yes, sir,' said the Pissa, backing away.

Evening came, and still no Silent girl. Dragging his feet, he joined up with the night's crew. Six, Forty, two of those other runts from block D. The battery block was a low, flat building, painted an ugly green that was somewhere between khaki and the color of hospital insides. Dark stalls promised the stench of acid.

'Shit job,' said Forty.

'Truth,' he agreed.

With a grunt, Forty hooked up the heavy green hose, and Six turned on the water, and they began. From long experience they knew not to approach until Forty was done with the first round of hosing down; when the big child put down the hose, they dove in, squelching, scrubbing brushes scraping rough metal cases, breathing into handkerchiefs tied over their faces. The Pissa worked in grim silence, trying not to breathe in, trying not to see.

Presently something hit him in the back of the head. He cried out and swung a slap at whoever was behind. He hit Forty.

'What did you do that for?' he cried.

They were going to scuffle, right there in the battery block, but the other two stepped between them and pulled them apart. The Pissa held his arms up, palms out. Peace. Forty growled and slapped them away. The Pissa stood there, confused, and another stone struck him. This time on the shoulder, from the direction of the wall. There was a scrabbling noise.

They all turned. There, silhouetted in the moonlight, was a head. It was Silent girl.

'Stupid new friend,' said Forty.

Silent girl mimed furiously. Come-come.

'One minute,' said the Pissa urgently to the others. Forty let him pass with a scowl.

She was standing on the broken road, a long stick in hand. Behind her loomed the hulks of old buildings, turned shades of black and brown by the darkness.

'Can't leave until I'm done here,' he said as he approached her.

She held up a finger for silence.

He peered down at her and whispered. 'Where were you? I was looking for you all day!'

She sniffed at him, no doubt catching the stench of the battery acid, then waved her hands. Irrelevant. She jabbed downward.

'Eh?' he said, squatting to see better. There, in the dirt, were stick figures. People. One taller than the others. Adult.

She tapped the children, pointed at him, then her.

He hunted for words. 'Nice.'

She shook her head. Tapped the Adult. Pointed behind him.

In the moonlight he could make out Kanishkersir's tent. 'Kanishkersir? That's Kanishkersir?'

Nod.

'Okay, good art?'

She threw up her hands in frustration and pointed to another set of squiggles in the dirt. He squinted.

Children.

With spears.

Children killing each other. Some stick figures lay flat on the ground. And there were two adults, standing behind the lines of children.

She peered at him expectantly.

'I don't understand,' he said. 'I don't know what this is. Where's your Radio?'

'Oy! Thirteen!' came Forty's voice, carrying low but clear through the night.

'You coming in?' the Pissa said, suddenly tired and irritated.

He saw the frustration on Silent girl's face. She pounded the ground with her fist. But nothing was worth the punishment for skipping battery duty. He leaned over and held out both hands; she scuffed the drawings with her foot and jumped up.

'You okay?'

She shook her head, jabbed at his chest, shook her head again. Not-okay. You-not-okay.

'Tell me in the morning?'

She shrugged.

He didn't know what to make of that, so he turned his back and trudged back to the stench. Nothing was worth skipping battery duty.

When he turned back, she was already gone.

EIGHT

The Pissa, thought Silent girl for the umpeenth time, was an idiot.

He had always been a bit stupid, but she'd taught him the ways of the street, and he had held his own in Colombo 3. Now she watched him with the others; working with them, sitting with them, eating with them, becoming slower, stupider ...

Less vigilant.

She was dimly aware now that there were different types of children. The Adults had called her an Explorer. The big one was a Builder. There were others in Colombo 3 who were not here, some sorts she had not put into words, but knew for their abilities: some who could command, some who could endure, some who could fight well. Perhaps the Pissa was of a different type, one whose biggest skill was ...

The huge one they called Forty guffawed, slapping the Pissa so hard on his back some of the food spilled off his plate. Once the Pissa would have driven a knee into the older child's stomach and a sharp thumb into his neck. Now he just looked stunned and, a slow second later, started to laugh with his tormentor.

... Belonging. Maybe his biggest skill was belonging.

If so, it was pathetic.

She turned from the sight, walking swiftly, her head down, a paper parcel in her arms.

Two minutes to make sure no one was looking, And then she tossed the parcel over the wall.

Another minute. A guard with a gun turned her way. She pretended to keep walking. He turned back. In a thrice she was over the wall, running to the parcel, dodging into the darkened hulks on the other side of the street.

She had the way memorized now. Left – right – down the stairs here – right again – straight ahead. A gaping cave-mouth yawned ahead of her, all rust and steel fringed with whatever remained of the building that had birthed it. She rapped on the side of the entrance, knuckles sharp against the metal.

In the gloom, a face appeared. The Burnt girl.

The Silent girl knelt and unwrapped the bundle. Gray clothes. These she slipped on. Food, stolen from Kanishkersir's personal tent, embossed with the logo of two mountains and a neat stamp saying 'Made in Kandy'. They were by far the best food she had ever had in her life. The Pissa had said they weren't for the children to eat, but Burnt girl liked them.

She handed one of the packet meals to the Burnt girl, who pulled out a wicked-looking knife from somewhere and cut off the top. The Burnt girl had no gun, had no truck with them; the knife was her dominion.

They gobbled the food in short, sharp bites, eyes darting around, pausing every so often to cock their ears at something. Someone looking at them would have seen something more animal than human in the way they ate. Then, when it was done, the Burnt girl stepped aside and nodded her in.

'Good luck again,' she said, that beautiful voice emerging from a cracked and twisted visage.

The Silent girl nodded, partly in thanks, partly in respect. Winning the friendship of Burnt girl had not been easy. Some people had to be treated with caution and politeness.

She moved on.

The tunnels were damp, and dark, and things slithered and crawled in here in the dark, but the tunnels also went to many places. The path they had taken to get here when they first arrived – and she had that route clearly traced out in her mind – was just one.

It had taken her many weeks to coax the Burnt girl to show her the others, but eventually food and company had won her over. Nobody spoke to the Burnt girl. Nobody understood how much the Burnt girl wanted them to speak to her.

The Silent girl moved in the darkness, the old pipe-tunnel clanging dully.

Left. Straight. Right. Straight. Up. Here. The air was fresher here. Up again. There were spikes in the walls – all that was left of an iron ladder welded in a shaft running from the ground right down into the tunnels. She began to climb.

The world she emerged in was very different from the Halfway House. The house was made up of quiet, and nice roads, and brick walls. This was a place of dirt and graves and long metal houses on wheels that burned and screamed. There were two on either side of her, matted with grease, perched on tracks of metal. One of them growled, a long, shuddering, many-throated growl that was almost defeaning. It was like rain on a metal rooftop, except louder, more beastial. There was a strange smell in the air, like fresh flowers had been mixed with death.

Thankfully, whoever had built these things had put ladders everywhere. She was up and over in the blink of an eye, snaking around linkages and coils and metal plates. A long concrete platform, shot through with ugly metal pillars and gray metal benches, stretched out before her. She clambered on top.

'Welcome to Colombo Fort Railway Station,' said a voice, low and female and blurred by the noise of the train. 'Travelling without a ticket is prohibited.'

She sat and waited.

Presently where was a tide of people. A gray wave, chattering, moving; hands reaching for boxes, bottles, things she didn't quite understand. She dove in, walking with the rest of them, trying to ape their movement, their gestures; trying to blend in with the gray. If anyone met her eyes she looked away.

Soon the train was empty. It whistled from somewhere far out of sight. There was a great clank and a shudder, and the metal beast began slowly pulling away from the station. She had a vague, cloudy memory; of sitting here and watching it move all the way out of sight; she knew that it went faster and faster, and sometimes crushed careless children underneath it.

'That's Lot one marked,' said an Adult who was lounging lazily on one of the metal seats. He waved a hand. 'Have a drink, charge your batteries, get back to work.'

Someone carefully opened up one of the boxes and began passing out cans. She pocketed hers.

And she was out.

Colombo 1 hit her in a riot of noise and smell. More people than had any right to co-exist walked past her in an endless monotone of gray. Faces, faces everywhere. Buildings loomed over them, lit up with color and neon that, in the evening light, changed the crowds as they walked underneath, blue-pink-purple-gray blue-pink-purple-yellow.

She looked back at the railway station. It gleamed white. She set off.

If there was one good thing about the Grays, it was that they didn't pry, or perhaps they didn't care. As long as she kept her head down she could go anywhere. She did so now, following the crowd upstream towards the mountain of rubbish that rose in horizon. She passed the market with its riot of colors and scents, breathing in, preserving the scent in her lungs.

It made her skin crawl, being close to this many people, but this particular place was beautiful: a sprawl of stalls and huts and colors, where children brought things they had made, and gave them to Adults, and took other things in exchange, things of light and color and smell. Sometimes even food. She passed an exchange where children lined up, clutching small things, and left with clothes of many colors.

With a jolt, she realized that some of the small things were hands, feet, eyes, hair: parts of dead children.

She hurried away.

A pack of children stood outside the market, listening to a taller child standing on a box. He held aloft a sign. She couldn't read it, but it was red and angry.

She drifted slowly towards him, trying to make out what he was saying. It was rushed, and very strange, but she caught the words 'Halfway House!' and 'Burn!'

'Burn!' chanted a few children closest to the box. Most of them just stared.

'Burn!' screamed the child again. 'If they won't put down their guns and give us back our land, burn them!'

'Burn them!' repeated the children closest to him. 'Burn all!'

She ignored them. Children had always screamed and would always scream. She crossed the street and kept walking until she came to the building with the hand outside. Above it hung a white banner, with crude black words inked on it: Ministry of Reconciliation.

There was a strange feeling around this place. It was in the way the children stood around it, silent and alert, unlike the blissfully unaware idiots at the market not so far away. They were a gang: they didn't look like one, not in their dull gray, but she had seen enough of gangs to know that shared body language, the way they moved with familiar, intimate rudeness, watching the rest of the world but not each other.

The sense of wrongness grew. It was the vehicles parked outside – white vans, unloading boxes, more than there had been the last time. From the white vans they lifted barrel after barrel of angry red, and then sharp things – spears, not like the ones she made, but brighter and more cruel; and other things that screamed of death and pain. These vans moved, too, unliked the ones back home. Every time a van emptied it would pull away with a slow growl and be replaced by another.

One of the children at the vans looked her way, and she saw what she had expected: dead eyes, like the children with the guns.

As she made her way back to the train station, she saw the boxes they had been unloading. They were open, and she saw the black gleam of guns inside. Ten children carefully lifted the guns, wrapped them in towels and passed them into vans that stood waiting outside, back doors open, headlights grinning yellow in the dark.

'Alright, that's Lot Twenty Seven, everyone take a break!' shouted the lazy adult, who was still lounging in his metal seat. 'Next train arrives at dawn!'

She watched for as long as she dared, and slunk away, uneasy. Something bad was about to happen, and she had to make the Pissa understand before it was too late. But when she got there, the Radio didn't have the words, and the Pissa couldn't understand what she drew in the sand.

≈

There came a day when Kanishkersir ordered them all out of their houses.

It was a gray day, with clouds like pillows under a strangely dark sky. He made them spread out and start digging – not the wide, sloping holes for planting, but the long, narrow kind, in threes and twos. The guards came and planted long poles and fit them together like pyramids of metal bones. At the top of each was a glassy black thing that moved on its own with a soft whirr and would turn to look at whoever was nearby. It was new to the children, but the Pissa frowned: he had seen similar things. Above the automated guns in Colombo 3. They were what let the guns see whom to shoot at.

Out of the corner of his eye he saw Silent girl. She crouched in the shade, watching them. He waved to her and turned back to his digging.

Presently Kanishkersir strolled out and surveyed the scene with great satisfaction.

'Right. Brilliant,' he said. 'All of you, stand there.'

Obediently, they clustered near the entrance. The black cameras whirred and looked at them.

'You too!' said Kanishkersir, motioning to Silent girl. She approached warily, her spear still clutched in her hand, and crouched down in front of them. The adult made a sort of square with his hands and peered at them through that. He was evidently pleased by what he saw.

'Great,' he said. 'Perfect lighting, perfect.' He cocked his head to one side, as if listening to someone they couldn't see. 'Kandy Center Four, are you getting the feeds? Right. Good. We're streaming on low bandwidth at the moment. Just a test.'

Whatever he was listening to made his smile a little bit wider.

'You lot, go get some sleep,' he said, motioning carelessly at the children. 'You've got a big day tomorrow.'

They dispersed, puzzled. The Pissa turned to go with Forty and the others, but found his hand gripped in small, iron-like fingers. Silent girl dragged him gently out of sight.

Come-with-me, she mimed, pulling him back to their house. On the floor were two small packs – cloth tied with rope – and her Radio. She gave him one and held up the Radio.

'I need you to come this way,' crackled the Radio in a man's voice. She pressed the button again and the voice repeated the urgent plea. And again.

'Okay, okay, coming.'

She signed. No-noise. Mouth-shut.

He rolled his eyes, but followed her anyway. They slipped past the houses, Silent girl moving from shadow to shadow, the long sharp spear held low and ready. For the first time he felt a tingle of apprehension.

She took him to the river-side of TRIPOLI, the overgrown yard where the wall was lowest.

Up-over.

'What?'

Up-over!

'The guards will catch us!'

She pointed to the guards, who were busy doing something to one of the cameras. Their guns hung by their sides.

'No! No!' he whispered at her, grabbing her hand.

She hissed in frustration, slapped his hand aside and tossed herself over the wall. Glancing around nervously, he followed. She was waiting for him on the other side of the road with that look on her face.

'You're being stupid,' he told her. 'I don't know what we're doing here.'

She pulled him into the darkness. How did she know the way? She motioned him on, ducking into and out of old houses and roads carved between the spaces where walls once stood. He recognized the route they were taking: it led to the tunnel.

He slowed a bit. He had taken the tunnel exactly twice in his life – both times when he was sent out to Colombo. Something about it unnerved him. Perhaps it was the long, dark, deep dampness of it; perhaps it was Burnt girl, with her hideously deformed face and long knives, keeping guard.

'I don't think this is a good idea,' he began.

And then he cleared a corner and saw her there; a girl in clothes the color of blood, standing in front of the gaping dark of the tunnel. She stood in the ruins of the mansion that housed the tunnel, surrounded by a webwork of light that streamed in through holes in the roof, lighting up that ghastly, dead-looking skin of hers. Silent girl was saying something to her, gesturing furiously. She was offering food. Packets and packets of biscuits and the new rations from Kanishkersir's tent.

Burnt girl saw him.

'You cannot pass,' she said. 'You stay on this side, the Colombo people stay on theirs. Nobody passes unless Kanishkersir tells me.'

Silent girl waved more food in her face. Burnt girl shook her head.

Silent girl pointed to herself, the food, then him, herself, him, the tunnel.

And still the Burnt girl blocked they path. She drew a knife, a long, curved, silvery thing that gleamed in the light.

As quick as a lightning flash, Silent girl flipped up her spear and rammed it into Burnt girl's chest.

They both stared at her in shock and disbelief, the Pissa and the Burnt girl. Silent girl drew her finger over her lips.

No noise.

The knife fell from Burnt girl's hand, and she collapsed. Silent girl knelt with her, throwing her weight on the spear. There was a crunch.

'You were different,' Burnt girl said, a look of disbelief still on her face.

Silent girl nodded and mimed. Sorry.

The red of the dress grew darker. A long slow whine escaped from Burnt girl's throat, and then she fell silent.

Silent girl bowed her head and began scooping up the food she had offered. The Pissa knelt to help her. Food. Packet meals of the kind Kanishkersir always ate. Water. She moved with speed, picking up the dead girl's knife and tossing it to him. He caught it, still stunned.

Come-come. She spared one last look at the dead girl lying with a spear in her chest, pale skin lit by crossbeams of light. Sorry, she mimed, disappearing into the darkness of the tunnel, heading away. They were halfway down the tunnel when the gunfire began.

She saw it in his face. His ears cocked. His face paled. His mouth opened. He made to dash past her, back the way they had come, but she stuck out her spear and he went sprawling in the wet rust-slime of the tunnel.

Something exploded behind them. From the direction of the Halfway House came a low, thin screaming, like a child in pain.

She held him down as he struggled, furiously strong in his panic, to run back, to join the guns.

'No!' he screamed at last. 'No! No! No!'

And he kept on screaming, even as she panted, trying to keep him down. Pop-pop-pop, went the guns. Something began pounding, a slow, deep thud that shook the walls of the tunnel.

Eventually he calmed down and started sobbing.

Something broke inside her, and she hugged him fiercely, no longer in a chokehold, but the fierce hug of one friend to another. But he had to understand.

Death, she signed. She mimed the guns firing and children falling. Death. Much death. She pointed to Colombo 1. Death from Colombo 1.

'Those are my friends,' he cried, not understanding.

She led him by the hand to one of the places where the tunnel peeked out: a half-broken cluster of buildings surrounding a little lake, ringed with steps on all sides. The tunnel-mouth was hidden from sight, in one of the few corners where one could peek out and not be seen from the main roads. There was a noise on the other side of the trapdoor – a precise, relentless pounding, like many feet hitting the ground.

From small shutters and holes they peeked out, and saw an army of gray-clad children, faces grim, feet pounding the ground, running towards the halfway ground in dreadful unison. In their hands they carried knives and guns. Adults strode among them, wearing the white shirts that said Ministry of Reconciliation on the back.

A shrill voice broke through, startling them:

'Burn!' it cried.

'Burn!' echoed a choir of child-throats, hideously beautiful. 'Burn the Halfway House!'

'Livestream online in five seconds,' said an awful Voice, cutting through the din.

'My friends,' whispered the boy seeing all this from behind the iron door of the tunnel.

She put her hands to his face and turned it towards her gently.

I am your friend, she signed. Come with me.

'Livestream online in one second,' said the Voice again. It bore a passing resemblance to the one who, in another life, had startled her with its talk of bluetooth, but this one was harsher, more menacing. 'Livestream online.'

She turned and ran through the tunnel, back to the route she knew and had prepared for. He followed, crying. After a while, she turned around and put her finger to her lips, and from then only his footsteps followed.

NINE

Meanwhile, in far-off Kandy, the sun rose over gray-brown hills, turning the misty night into a haze of gray and gold. It had done so long before the humans came and claimed these hills and set up their temples, and by now had gotten into the habit of things.

The Sacred City, too, having sat still in its own shadow for almost a thousand years, had gotten used to the sight. Only the watchtower, ever vigilant, moved; its solar cell arrays hummed gently, unfolding lotus-like from their slumber.

All was quiet.

It was a strange place, full of pain and bitterness and dreams and old as the mountains themselves. Many hundreds of years ago it had been a kingdom of its own, its paths guarded, its warriors swift to attack and retreat; and time and time again it had changed allies and crushed enemies until its supremacy was unrivalled, and its rulers wreathed themselves with pomp and tradition.

But there comes a tide in the affairs of men. It was Kandy that first invited foreigners to rule this land, and once its rivals lay shattered it soon realized the folly of its actions: for shut away in the mountains, with no access to the sea, facing armies of guns and warships with spears and bows, the Kingdom of Kandy had signed a death warrant upon the whole country.

By the time the British arrived, it was weak, and easily taken. It stayed taken, the Great Houses and families too obsessed with their own power and their own hills to unite and fight the enemy.

And when the Royal Maritime Society discovered the rich minerals that lay off the coasts of Ceylon – the thorium that powered London, the graphite that went into the processing cores of the Analytical Engines – the powers of Kandy descended from their mountains to find a world reduced to dust and ashes, and themselves little more than old and prideful servants under the eye of Her Majesty the Queen of England.

≈

A sudden wailing pierced the mist, accompanied by flutes, drums and an oddly repetitive snare.

'Muge ammata,' cursed one man, startled. He was lean and gray-haired and looked bone-tired, and also looked like he'd been quietly enjoying a nap.

'It's only that song, what's she called, Malini,' said one of younger assistants, unfazed.

'It's hideous.'

'You've heard it plenty of times before.'

'Still hideous,' grumbled Gray Hair. He scraped his tongue against his teeth, suddenly and intensely aware of how foul his mouth smelled. 'Alright, status?'

'Running fine, sir,' said an eager voice nearby. Another assistant. 'Combat zone cameras ready.'

'And the feed?'

'Broadcasting, sir. All normal.'

He clapped his hands, and suddenly the inside of the Watchtower went from a dull stone-gray carving to a fantastically detailed view of the Colombo Project. Colombos 3, 4, 5, 8 – and there was the huge mountain of garbage – and the glimmering Port City – and Colombo 1. 1 was a mass of gray ants marching.

The older man studied it. 'Show me Tripoli.'

The view moved, shifted, centered. Dull brick boxes shot through with straight lanes. Children with guns and spears crouched inside what was obviously the world's most useless fort.

'Looks normal.'

Assistant Two sat down and began tapping on the lightboard at her desk. 'Betting market's going crazy,' she reported idly.

'Who's betting?'

'The Bandaras are going all-in on the defenders this year,' said Two. 'Ratwatte, Rambukpotha all against. Madugalle split.'

'If I could bet, I'd take home the Bandara's bank accounts,' said Gray Hair. His name was Don Hewage, though nobody called him Don or Hewage: to most people he was simply 'sir'.

'Non-deterministic interactions, you can't predict,' said One.

'Watch me,' said Hewage.

The three of them watched the battle play out across the walls.

'Now the charge,' said Hewage.

Children in gray, screaming, charged the lines, and were shot down in waves.

'Now the Molotovs,' said Hewage.

'Two of the Adults are showing signs of anomaly, sir,' said Assistant One. 'Conversation logs show them talking about Kandy. Home. They're making bets with each other on who'll win.'

'Showing incentive,' said the cheerful assistant.

Assistant One shot her a look.

'One of them tried to investigate where the children come from.'

'And?'

'Humanitarian cause, I think. He definitely knows we're making them at the Port City. I had him recalled for questioning. The other was Kanishka.'

'Ah. That old hippie bastard. Recall him when the livestream is done. Give him his paycheck and send him home.'

On the big screen, burning bottles were tossed, setting parts of the defender's rudimentary fortress on fire. Assistant One conceded defeat. The defenders were being run over by waves and waves of children. They climbed over the stacked bodies of the dead and were mowed down, set fire to, and speared.

'Bingo,' said Hewage.

'If this goes on we might have to double the Port City production for the next cycle,' observed Assistant One. He paused, checked something. 'Remember that Explorer unit that crossed the mountain border?'

Hewage grinned. 'Changing the subject, eh? Explorer? I take it she's dead?'

'Not really. Her ID tag's actually showing from somewhere in the battle. Still alive.'

A rare, slow smile briefly flitted across Hewage's face. 'The Explorers were always different,' he said. 'Fabulous piece of work. Perfect loner, moves away from crowds, sticks to the edges. Without them we'd never have known of those early break points. What was she doing in this mess?'

'She seems to be travelling with a newer-generation Connector, sir. Might explain why she's among the camps.'

'Keep an eye on them, but there's no reason to worry. They'll be flushed and rebuilt anyway. You make sure the connection doesn't drop. And keep track of damage.'

'Anything I can do, sir?' piped in Two.

Hewage thought about it. 'You make sure the networks get the feed and do their edits properly,' he said. 'We don't want the monks complaining about body parts all over the place again. I'm going back to sleep.'

≈

Meanwhile, surrounded by the noise and the charnel stink of death, the two children climbed up a tunnel and emerged, blinking, on the Colombo Fort station.

It was empty. No trace remained of the gray-suited children and Adults who thronged this place. All that remained was the platform, silent, and the gleaming tracks, and the hot sun, and the train, black and grumbling gently.

'Departure in fifteen minutes,' said a disembodied voice.

The boy flinched, but the girl pushed him up, throwing out their spears, her radio, their flimsy backpacks. She hauled herself up last and pushed him behind the train. There they crouched, teeth bared, listening intently.

Nothing.

'What do we do now?' said the Pissa.

The train muttered; the pitch of its engines shifted ever so slightly upwards.

She swung herself up into the carriage and beckoned for him to follow.

'What are you doing?' he asked, even as he let himself be dragged into an empty carriage.

The girl sighed. Very carefully, she rummaged through her tapes, selected three and played them at the Pissa.

'This place isn't safe.' CLICK. 'We need to get out of here.' CLICK. 'Follow me.'

'We're going on the train? Where does this go to?'

How could she explain that this train went to the Kandy they all talked about? She knew the trains. She knew the timing. She thought about it and selected three more tapes.

'Yes.' Click. 'I don't know.' Click. 'To a better place.'

'My friends are all dying,' he said quietly. He sounded like he was about to cry.

She waited.

Eventually he understood, as she hoped he would. The Pissa wasn't stupid, but this place had made him soft. She reached out and touched his cheek, gently, and pulled him towards the next carriage, where it was darker and there was less chance of them being seen.

'Departure in ten minutes,' said the voice.

It waited a bit, and tried again. 'Departure in five minutes. Please make sure all cargo, passengers and luggage are stores and accounted for.'

Nobody replied. In the distance there was smoke and the faint sound of children screaming.

Humming to itself, the train revved up its engines, and, with a great clank and a thud, began the long journey out of Colombo Fort, taking the two survivors with it.

TEN

The train, the Pissa found, was a strange thing. At first he'd been frightened of the way it moved, the way the ground seemed to pass by in a blur of speed when it screamed: it seemed impossible that something so large could travel so fast. It was like being inside a living thing, with its roar out front and a heartbeat that spoke in carriages bumping against each other.

'Where are we going?' he asked her.

Away, she signed back. She had been watching the train for weeks now. How it moved and stopped and spoke by itself. How it would stop at places. How it felt almost safe inside.

Surely this was better than waiting to be killed by the gray people. She remembered the children marching, and shuddered. They settled for sitting in an empty carriage, watching the smoke rise and the burning flame of Colombo 01 pass them by.

She nestled back in the darkness and tried reading the map again, the one she'd found on the side of the passenger compartment. It was like paper, but also reminded her of those lights outside the market. And it was glass and metal and did not bend. If she touched it in certain places it would flash and make a sound. It showed one thing, and one thing only: a small map of Colombo, and on it, a Line, and moving on the line, a blinking dot.

She was sure the dot was them. Every so often other labels would come up. When it said 'Maradana' on the map the train had swung by a sun-dried set of buildings the color of old bones left in the sun. Two flags hung everywhere – one a colorful gold and red with some kind of animal holding something sharp, the other green with a crescent-moon shape on it. 'Maradana Railway Station,' read dead neon tubing. She could not read the letters, but she did understand the patterns. She knew what 'railway station' meant.

The train did not stop, but passed through at a steady clip. She craned her head outside, wondering if people lived in those old-bone buildings.

Thus, lost in her own reverie, it was quite some time before she heard the banging.

It was a loud sound, harsh and metallic. If she could have guessed it would have been the sound of someone banging hard on a metal door; like the time Forty had been locked up for doing something wrong. It was a heavy sound.

Silent girl shook the Pissa awake and held a finger to his lips for silence.

The sound was coming from two boxes down the line. He understood.

Slowly they crept towards the door, hands on their spears.

The banging did not cease. There was the sound of a voice outside the door, but it was tiny and sounded like it is coming from a speaker far past its prime.

Slowly the two children crept up to it, falling into their old formation: him in front with her at the back with the spear.

They waited for long time for the banging to go away, but it didn't. At some point he looked back at her and she nodded and he opened the door.

And recoiled with fright.

ELEVEN

Many decades ago old Ceylon had been home to a curious phenomenon: the conductor. Most often found in buses, the conductor was a curious life form: his life – for it was always him and not her – revolved around cramming as many passengers as humanly and inhumanly possible into a small metal box and demanding their money. Then came a time when this skill set was found uniquely adaptable to the train system.

But time passes and flesh is replaced with steel. What the children saw then was a holdover from the days when people remembered conductors but no longer remember them being human.

It was a broad and unpleasant thing with many arms from which dangled what had once been checklists: an empty slot for a mouth served as a ticket printer.

And above this loomed ugly red eyes set in a face that looked like a thin and starving demon, flame-like protrusions where its ears should have been: an old *yakmuna*, a devil mask, carved in metal and given life.

It loomed over them, taller than any adult they had ever seen.

'Tickets,' it demanded of them in a faint and reedy voice. Two of its arms were held out like claws. 'Tickets!'

The children backed away slowly, fear fighting wonder in their hearts. Never before had they seen anything like this.

The Conductor took a step forward. And another. And another.

'Unauthorized travellers will be subjected to the full penalty of the law,' it intoned gleefully. 'Go to the front!'

There was no time for thought. They fled, shrieking. There was no other word for it. In all of their lives they had never seen anything like this before, and their fists and legs pumped in the pure, primal panic of children. They ran helter-skelter through the dock and rumbling carriages, fleeing from the mental thing that ran behind them, 'Thud, thud, thud, thud...'

At first it seemed like they were winning. Their nimble bodies sneaked easily between the seats and the doors and the rumbling metal gears, outpacing the giant that hunted them.

But little children cannot run forever. The boy huffed and hissed as he ran. The girl stumbled with her spear: It kept getting caught in the seats.

Two of the great clawed arms reached out for them and caught them. They screamed and reached out for doors and seats and anything they could grab, but the metal arms were relentless: they pulled the children back as if they were nothing.

'Tickets?' it demanded.

The Pissa felt the cold, hard clamp on one wrapping itself around his rib cage, choking the breath out of him.

The girl screamed, a wordless, shrill shriek, and hit it with the spear. Sharp jabs, to the eyes, to the face. The spear just slid off and clattered to the floor. The grip around her body tightened and she screamed some more.

'Unauthorized travellers will be subjected to the full penalty of the law,' said the awfully scratchy voice of the train conductor. 'To the front!'

And it began marching forward, plowing through the seats, dragging the two children with it.

'Let me go,' screamed the boy at the robot. 'Let me go let me go let me go!'

The conductor paid him no heed, but pulled them relentlessly forward. The girl struggled against it, and it swung ever so gently to the side, holding her aloft; the edge of a baggage rack hit her right in the head and she gave a little cry of surprise and was silent, her eyes closed.

But in the act of leaning to the left, the conductor showed the Pissa something that had never been meant to be seen: a little gash, a little opening near the neck, in which something sparked and sparkled. In that brief glimpse , the Pissa saw so many things moving: things that turned things that went up and down. And then it was gone again hidden as the metal sheet that was the collarbone of the conductor slid over it, as it was supposed to.

They came to a halt in front of a particularly large metal door.

'Warning: Units Cannot exceed Class-3 damage to passengers,' a speaker rebuked the robot.

The Conductor made a scratching noise. 'Unauthorized travellers will be subjected to the full penalty of the law,'

Its neck shifted again, revealing that sparking gash in the metal.

The Pissa didn't understand what he saw: but he understood whatever it was was something Important to the metal creature. He had seen sparks like this once before, when the girl used the wires trailing from an old gun to light a fire, and when children died.

His mind raced. His arms scrabbled uselessly at the sides. His knife was too far out of reach, strapped to his leg but his left hand came up holding his screwdriver – the one. He threw it at the machine, hoping to have the same spot that had just revealed itself to him.

It bounced harmlessly just off the back.

The conductor paused. Its head, that thin demon's mask, turned around quizzically. And in doing so the opening showed itself again.

His hands scrabbled furiously at his sides again. Knife...knife...

'Damage to train property will not be tolerated,' it hissed, raising a metal claw.

The Pissa's hands came across his water bottle: leaking, punctured by the cracks and repeated bashings against the seats. It was not a knife. His heart sank with panic.

'Units cannot exceed Class-3 danger to passengers,' warned the voice from the train.

The conductor hesitated. And in that moment, the boy, held aloft, reached out in pure desperation and jammed the leaking water bottle into the opening in the conductor's neck.

'Damage to...' began the Conductor.

And something made a noise inside its body, a noise like thunder caught in a bottle, and its glowing eyes dulled. Its hands opened: the two children fell to the ground with an unceremonious crash. The metal automaton, black smoke drifting out of its neck, shuddered.

'Damage to train property. Train. Train. Train. Property.'

The devil mask groaned.

'To the front,' it said, one last time, and was silent.

When the girl came to, it was to an unexpected softness. Below her, around her.

Metal rails danced in front of her. She used one of them to haul her body upwards and looked around, confused.

She was lying in a train carriage: not the one they'd left, but, from the looks of it, something further up. A trail of destruction swept both sides, as if something huge and heavy had barged through the door and ripped its way past the rows and rows of blue seats. The stuffing had been pulled from one of these seats: she wondered if that was what she was sitting on right now. It felt so soft.

Her head hurt. She touched it. Her hands came away wet.

There was a loud noise. She ducked instinctively, her hands looking for a weapon. A moment later the Pissa poked his head around the seat and was almost brained by a heavy plastic thing.

He rubbed his head and looked at her reproachfully. Hands-up, palms-up, she apologized. What-happened? She mimed at him. The last thing she could remember was that metal monster dragging them both screaming to the front of the train.

He dropped what he was carrying onto her lap – tins of fuel biscuits, little packets of water and oil and other things that she didn't quite recognize. They leaned around the edge of the seat and he pointed at something a few carriages up. The doors were open and she caught a glimpse of a devil mask and a metal hand, lying on the ground.

'One of the carriages has the food store,' he said proudly, 'I got your food. You should eat, then we'll go explore.'

They ate, two children consumed by tiredness and thirst and hunger, oblivious of all else except the rocking of the train and of each other.

After a while he took her to see the rest of the train. There a trail of dropped tins and splashes of great and oil through one of the carriages, which had no seats: she assumed this was where he had found the food. And a little further, through the broken doors, there lay the metal monster. It knelt against the seat in an awkward surrender. Oil gleamed around its knees and her spear was plunged deep into its neck tilting the head almost comically aside.

It would have been funny, if this hadn't been the same metal monster that had picked them up so effortlessly and drawn them with such force through the train. As it was, there was something important about it: the empty devil mask seemed to leer at them.

The Pissa explained, in so many words, how he had first used water and then when the machine twitched, he had gone back for her spear and sunk it right through its neck. It was clear he was very proud of this. She said nothing, but hugged him and ran her eyes and hands over the strange thing, wondering what it was.

How did it move? Why did it look so much like an adult, and yet so different?

Whatever it was, its journey had been terminated by a large metal door, quite unlike the others they had just passed. Over the years, she had come to understand doors, and what it took to breach them. Not even the Sons of Cinnamon could have broken through this one. There was a green light shining on it. She reached out to touch it.

'Warning: Unauthorized entry,' said a loud voice from around them. 'Passengers and robotics are prohibited from entering the driving module.'

It had no hint of threat about it: in fact, it was very much like the voice that once had told her that the Bluetooth device was ready to pair; but she drew back. She had left her radio, so she mimed to the Pissa – are-there-any-others?

'Not from here to there,' he said, pointing from where they stood right now to where they had come from.

We-have-food, we-have-water? She mimed again. Enough-for?

'A long time,' he said.

Good. Very good. She pointed to where he had gotten the food. We stay there. We defend that place.

He agreed. Always find the food and water, always defend the food and water. It was how Colombo survived.

She looked down at the devil mask again, and stamped on it with sudden savagery, cracking it. After a while he joined into, and the little children jumped up and down on the last Ceylonese conductor until its face was shattered and it lay in pieces.

≈

In the watchtower, in Kandy, the second Assistant bent over a notification.

'The Conductor on the Train Two just shut down,' she said.

'What's the problem?' said Assistant One, who was eating his lunch. 'Nucleus motor stuck again?'

Assistant Two frowned. 'No, that's odd, he's reporting attack,' she said. 'Unauthorized robotics on the train. Two of them.'

Assistant One shrugged. 'Must have been a glitch,' he said. 'Maybe it finally went mad and tried swinging a fist at the kids. You know how those things are.'

'He wouldn't have gone *mad,*' said Assistant Two. 'I told you we should have sent someone down for maintenance a long time ago.'

'You and those old robotics,' scoffed Assistant One, and went back to his eating his lunch. It was home-cooked rice and chicken curry and excellent enough to keep a man from doing the work he was paid to do.

TWELVE

And thus it was that a train rolled gently across the blighted landscape of Ceylon, or Taprobane, or Lanka, carrying two lost little children. Someone looking would have seen them peer out through the windows from time to time: a quick flash of grimy brown skin and eyes.

They soon left the outskirts of Colombo behind. Before long the city and its smoke were a dot on the horizon. They passed Kelaniya, which had once been a thriving hotbed of religious and student revolt: now it was home to corpses, both human and robot, hung from creepers of wire like Christmas decorations, long since dessicated or rusted. A red hand marked each of them.

They saw the radiation zone of Ragama, where buildings that had once been hospitals vomited a vile green into the moss that clung onto them, and great war machines stood gutted with their innards blown apart.

The train curved slowly through idle, overgrown fields. It took them to Gampaha, where people with rotting flesh and too many toes and fingers wailed at the approach of the great black beast and threw flowers at it, praying for it to go away; their prayers were answered, for the train paid them no heed, but rumbled on. And at last the corpses and the rust gave way to tough grass and flowers, and stone arches and beautiful bridges, and the clear sky peeked out past the clouds.

And there was no one to see except for the children, save for the sentry turrets that looked at the train and looked back, resuming their old vigil. They had seen this many times before.

≈

In Kandy, the second Assistant had just finished her shift. The Watchtower, that nexus which looked out over the hills, had fallen silent, save for her footsteps. Evening had taken over the gray-brown city outside, turning it into shades of ash and dust.

She looked at the screens for one last time. The livestream had ended. Now they displayed a map of Colombo 1 with red splattered all over it. One side declared kill counts: the other viewer numbers.

They had not broken any records this season, but come close. Thousands dead, millions watching.

The elevators took her down there, scaling the towering gray building; through the glass doors the horizon slowly rose, until she was among steel walkways and scaffolding, and then the labs, one after the other: huge plants where machines and humans pieced together the children they sent out into the wild set-stages of Colombo.

Usually the sight excited her. Today it did nothing of the sort. She walked through the slow narrow streets of Kandy. The sky was a dull gray overhead, and on this day like on most days, it sent to her a little beats of music in raindrops. Pitter patter pitter patter, they went, dancing a tune on the cobbles on the windows, and on herself, a slow rhythm that only she could hear.

Like on most days, her thoughts were at work; her mother had always said that she thought too much about work for women. Today she thought about her colleague and Hewage, that old gray haired bastard, who kept belittling her, who kept sidelining her thoughts as if she hadn't studied the same things they did, as if she hadn't worked as hard if not harder to get to where she was.

But why do you even need to go to work? Her mother used to ask. We'll find you a husband. He will provide for you. They have to. All you have to do is sit and enjoy the house and what more could a human ask for?

She didn't have the heart to tell her mother that she liked the work, as gruesome as it was. Watching the children slaughter each other over and over again, even if they weren't children – even if it disturbed her sometimes, it also fascinated her beyond measure, beyond her mother's cooking recipes and the matriarch's gossip about men. The way no battle was the same. How simple effects – a blocked alley here, a couple of hundred more units here, a Tribe disrupt there – let to such complex effects.

And they watched it, didn't they? All the high bloods and the low castes, they all huddled around the TVs every six months, making bets, having arguments, setting crackers on fire and sharing drinks with complete strangers as they watched the oil being shed.

She had heard that things were different. Once there had been something called cricket, involving a wooden bat and a ball – though for the life of her she couldn't understand why people would watch men throw balls at each other. But there were records: photos: of people chanting, cheering, waving their flags high. People of all nations and all colors. And there was a time, said the books, when no caste or no religion could get between Ceylonese and their cricket.

People like a show, she thought. They'll clap, of course they will they laugh and cry over men swinging bits of wood around, but take that away from them and they'll just find something else to laugh at.

Her feet, completely unobservant of what her head was thinking, took her past determines and the twists and the little puddles the children jumped into and brought her to the house.

The emblem of the Ceylon Planters Rifle Corps was embossed on the metal door: her father had always stayed true to the army.

She pushed open the steel grill paused in front of the lens, and waited. Pretty soon their servant, anaging woman of dark swarthy skin and a harried look, opened the the great double-blind steel door. She had always felt it a little too pretentious to have one servant to open the door, especially when most families used automated systems, but her father assured her that this was how they did it in the old times for me: and after all, did the Bandaras also not have servants?

Their family may not be as old, but they could bloody well afford it. And her mother, who saw the use in these little things, always agreed. It had once been the fashion to have a suitably low-class servant, either Indian or Tamil, and it might be again.

She pushed past the servant into the hall, where her brother was glued to the screen, and walked slowly up the stairs. Her brother said something to her, something about some fancy rich boy wanting to meet her, perhaps to ask her hand in marriage, but she let herself into the darkness of her old room and forgot everything except for her work.

She always did.

≈

Hewage went home too. His path took him through the city center, clustered around the gleaming lake, but also took him away from it, towards the hills and over them, through narrow lanes overlooking mountaintops. He saw men with dark skin, bent under the weight of the loads they carried, unprotected by plastic hazmat raincoats; they passed by him in silence, moving aside every so often to let him pass. His road took him to a small, modest homestead white concrete banded with iron and with a simple lead laced roof instead of the water tanks of the rich. He waved his ID and the door clicked open.

A small bundle of legs and head shrieked and buried herself in his belly. He laughed, as he always did, and lifted his daughter Heidi and swung her around, and she laughed too. He smiled faded a little bit when he saw his wife standing just behind.

'Husband,' she said.

'Wife,' he said. It was a simple ritual, no more than muscle memory now.

They watch their daughter run laughing into the other room.

'School fees arrived,' she said. 'Way overdue.'

'I know,' he said. 'I'm trying.'

And as he sat down to dinner with them as his fingers walked through the rice and curry and turn them into little balls for his daughter, he tried not to think about all those children dying, screaming, burning.

The gray sky swirled and nabbed, and the rain pattered down, bringing the soft, deadly radiation with it.

Only the sky could see the train, moving steadfastly forward towards Hewage and the second Assistant and Kandy, bringing with it two children who sat glued to the windows of the train, watching in awe as the landscape unfolded, unaware of the trouble they brought with them.

≈

Silent girl had watched the vegetation for a while, marveling at all that green, but every so often they would pass a station and she would be reminded that this train, at some point, had to stop. And after a while, she became aware that the stations were no longer deserted.

'Look! People!' said the Pissa, and fell silent.

Adults.

Adults were problems. They were darker than the ones she had seen, and bent in two; they carried heavy bags on their backs, and as the train passed, they peered at it with dull eyes. Without power armor they were thinner, almost fragile-looking: but she did not want them seeing her.

She dragged the Pissa by the arm to the map entombed in glass in the passenger compartments.

His lips moved as he tried to work it out.

'We're here,' he said, jabbing at a point halfway between Colombo and Kandy.

Halfway there. The Girl's squinted at the tiny photos of Kandy plastered next to the dot. Mountains: some kind of golden, glowing house. Water. Lots of water, like a small sea. It told her nothing.

She dragged her Radio out and started rummaging. The concept of readiness was difficult. She had tapes for being okay, she could mime many things, but...

She tried miming people opening the doors, coming in, killing them. She mimed them hiding. She ripped a piece of covering from her seat, wrapped it around her arm. Shield. She mimed a spear. Stab.

'Will they be...?' he asked carefully.

She tapped Colombo. Stab. Fire. Death.

The Pissa's face fell, and for a moment she saw something that might have been terrifying on a child's face; but she had spent her entire life surrounded by such faces, and deep inside she felt something ease into place. At last he understood.

Stab. Fire. Death.

Never again.

With new eyes they looked around, looking at things the way they had in Colombo.

≈

An hour later, a single black train pulled into the Kandy railway station. It was a holiday, and the station was critically understaffed, but the switches, having done this many times before, shunted the train neatly onto the track closest to the one railway operator on duty. He heard it coming and dialed the usual number.

'32-11, inbound, maintenance, clear,' he rattled off.

'32-11, alright,' said the voice at the other end. 'Crew's a bit late today, give me thirty minutes. Any damage?'

The operator spared a glance. 'No,' he said, bored, and hung up.

Just then, two things leaped into view. About four feet high. Metal gleamed and shone, wrapped in rough patches of cloth: it took him several seconds to recognize them as children from the Bloodsports. Through the glass panes he could make out gray-clothed limbs flapping, and – were those *seat covers* they were wearing?

They move bizarrely fast; there was a clank, and one of them snarled and thrust a metal pole at his box.

The operator started at the metal pole protruding into his body. Blood splurted out. The one who had stabbed him stepped into view.

It was a little robot, exactly like the ones you saw on TV: her face was a thin, bruised sliver of metal and plastic fakeflesh, the wire-hair matted and filthy, her hands scarred metal wrapped with cloth. Out of the corner of his eye he saw a taller robot running in, straight, metal held out like a javelin.

'Amme,' he said in disbelief, trying to redial. *'Ane AMME EPA...'*

He died before he could reach the phone.

≈

The two children stood over the fallen operator, contemplating.

The girl shrugged, pointing at what looked like the exit. Time to move on.

They did.

When the maintenance crew arrived twenty minutes later, they saw the operator. Two long, makeshift spears lanced through the flimsy metal-and-glass box he sat in, pinning the corpse to the glass. Red coated the inside and pooled on the floor. The putrid stink of blood and guts filled the place.

One of them puked. Another, so pale he looked like a corpse himself, pointed to the ground.

Two sets of bloody footsteps led away, towards the exit, disappearing into Kandy.

THIRTEEN

Thus it was that couple of months later, the second Assistant – she of Hewage's teching – found herself in the cold lab in the heart of Kandy, scalpel in hand, looking down upon the body of a dead robot.

It was a child. If it could be said to be a child. The little body, stretched out cold and bare, looked a lot like what God would have made the humans to look like had he been limited to metal and cheap plastic. Only the face looked human, and even there the artificial skin had peeled away, exposing the rusted metal underneath. There were bullet wounds in the little body where they had shot her, six of them. And out of these wounds flowed not blood, but a black ichor flecked and dusted with the silver of aluminum and bits of wire.

Six bullets to stop a child.

She had seen these things built, disassembled, cut up, and yet she found herself shivering. It was the eyes, she thought. They had gotten pretty good at designing eyes over the years..

'Shall we start?' said the disembodied voice on the speaker. Hewage sounded tired. He would be, she supposed. A whole mountain of crap had erupted, and was about to land on their heads.

Two bots had broken into Kandy, killed five men and two women, and when the private armies of the Kandy aristocracy had arrived with guns and violence, they came out, these two broken looking pitiful metal children, and pleaded for their lives, in a language they could barely understand: some debased Form of Sinhala mixed with Tamil.

And those men, who did usually very little but live on their masters wage and strut about in uniform, suddenly had to face the prospect of lining up and shooting something that screamed in pain. It wasn't the same as on TV.

And all eyes turned to the Ministry of Reconciliation, and demanded who was to blame. They would talk about this for centuries. Kandy, like the elephants of old, never forgot. The highest, who stood out easily, had been the first: but already the eyes were prying lower down the ladder, to the people who worked the shifts, to people like Hewage.

She shuddered and picked up the scalpel. The cadaver lay in front of her. She had read up on whatever Hewage had given her on the experimental models. Back when the Zone was first built they had deployed these to find the edges and the broken points, the ones they had used as guinea pigs to locate flaws in the Colombo warzone. The bot was built atypical, in the same way that some people were born tall or good-looking or with great hair.

They should have seen this coming. They should have seen something coming.

But first, the incisions. A grid along the back of the body. From the back it was an almost perfect reconstruction of a human being – except done in muscle-wire and steel. Here was the triangle of auscultation and the lumbar triangle: here the muscles traprezius and latissimus dorsi: here the iliac crest.

She peeled the fibre bundles apart, laying the flaps aside, and cut through the trapezius muscle, detaching from the spine. The muscles felt cold to the touch.

And here it was. Where the spinal accessory nerve should have been was a thin filament of optical wire, with roots that led deeper upwards and inwards. She followed cutting upwards to the suboccipital region, where four slender tensor muscle-wires protected the port interface. From here she could jack in and dissect the inner workings of the brain.

The port was shut. But this wasn't the slow damage of time – it was a perfect welded seal straight from the machine workshop.

'Ah shit,' said Hewage on the line. 'This is even older than I thought. Back when the old man had the idea for jacked-in upgrades but we hadn't figured them out yet.'

The software upgrades and the cyclical resets let the same avatars and the same bodies and the same neural networks fight each other, constantly learning from the experience, while not retaining too much of the memory about the lives that they had led and died and bled for.

'So this one's been active and unflushed all this time?'

'Apparently.'

Right. She first carefully finished dissecting the body, Popping the little arms out of their sockets, removing the power cells in the chest, disconnecting the legs and ripping out colds of wire and plugging them back into the computer.

She spoke into the recorder as she worked: never thinking too hard, never thinking about how small the body was, or how much it resembled all the children that she had grown up with: she let her surgeons instincts take over.

'Shrapnel embedded 2.3 inches into the main power supply,' she said. 'Blunt force trauma and grooves consistent with the sharp object visible across the right upper arm. The skin isn't holding the broken plates together, which might explain why the sargents said it favoured its left.'

'Hmm,' said Hewage. 'Right, continue. I'm making some calls. Submit the report as soon as you're done.'

He vanished.

Soon the body on the table no longer resembled a body on the table. Only the head had been left untouched.

Assistant-2 – Dr Almeida – sat down and stared at the face that looked serenely at her from the dissecting table.

She had thought long and hard about this: how terrified they must have been, both the children and the men. Had the children understood that not everyone had metal faces and hands of steel and plastic? Had they somehow automatically identified these flesh creatures as threats?

Because that was how their neural models were built: anything new was to be treated with suspicion and regarded as a threat unless proven innocent. And those men who shot them, did they not think in the same way? How did they look upon these childlike creatures that seemed so human and yet were not?

Working carefully, she disconnected the prefrontal cortex line and gingerly removed the head from the dismantled framework. The throat stuck: she turned it around, looking for the voicebox connections, but it had been sealed off from machine workshop. Whatever input reached it did not actually produce any sound at all.

Curious, she plugged it in and checked the communication protocols. In the place of the usual speech programming they installed, she found a series of hand signals and commands and references to what seemed like a store of external data. She remembered the reports again, that the child, no, robot, had died clutching a tape recorder in its arms.

Not for the first time, she felt a pang of pity for this creature, thrust into a strange and alien world without so much as a voice.

Just then, her phone started beeping. 'Event: Vows, 7 p.m. City Hall, Thirty Minutes.' it screeched at her.

'Day one log, ending,' she said to her recorder hurriedly, 'Initial investigation shows deviance from standard models. Possible factory modifications. Note: check communications modules tomorrow. Almeida out.'

'Event: Vows, 7 p.m.' repeated the phone.

Cursing slightly, she picked up her phone and rushed off to get dressed, leaving the broken robot corpse on the table.

≈

It was a distracted Almeida that made her way to the City Hall. The city, built on many slopes, curved gently down, and took her with it to the Hall. Strings of yellow bulbs hung from the trees, making the lake shimmer with the light of so many tiny artificial suns. Union Jacks sprouted from metal posts every so often, pointing the way.

The ordinarily deserted building was overrun that day with people in white; mostly civil servants – they had to be there – but also a health dose of anyone over twenty-one in Kandy. Like ants, people marched up the hexagonal steps, and settled down into pews in the great cathedral-like dome beyond, their whispers turning into a river of noise.

Almedia tried not to trip on the steps. She'd done her best with the saree and hoped it would pass muster.

It didn't, of course. There was only so much you could do in thirty minutes. The first wave of people she ran into were friends from school. They flocked to her like birds, adjusting her pins, straightening the saree, mouthing well-meaning but ultimately generic pieces of advice. She endured it, and extricated herself once the saree was laid out to proper Kandyan standards, leaving them to frown in disapproval at her disappearing back.

And she was in. The hall with its painted images loomed over her. The Buddha, preaching wisdom from his tree. The Kandyan surrender: the Sinhalese princes throwing down their arms at the feet of the painfully young, impossibly heroic-looking British officer. The Restoration: pomped-out British handing over the judiciary to Kandy's Buddhist temples. And, in the far back, almost in shadow, a painting of black-clad, monkish soldiers with long rifles in their hands, presiding over two naked Kandyans in chains, while a British Governer stood behind them.

The Inquisition. The legion of soldiers that stayed, and stayed, and never left. The Brit's most effective means of getting Kandy to toe the line.

She slipped into her seat.

It didn't take long to start. She couldn't see much over the heads of hundreds of people in front, but she heard the conch-shell, and the noise of drums, and the jangling clank of the ceremonial dancers as they carved a noisy path into the center of the hall. Following in their path was the perfect military clip-clop-clip precision of British soldiers. Most of them were probably Indian. Very few actual white men were put at risk in the colonies.

A softer, more metallic tread: the Gurkhas with their six-shooters and knives.

And lastly, a wave of almost perfect silence: the Inquisition. Only they broke the ceremony, walking not through the center, but from all around them, hooded monk-figures stalking through the pews, converging. Shivers spread through the crowd of assembled Kandyans wherever an Inquisitor passed. One swept past her: she had a brief glimpse of a pale face with ruby lenses for eyes, a brutal-looking hunting rifle slung over the shoulder.

She shuddered and zoned out, still thinking about the robot in her office.

A British officer unrolled a scroll and began to speak. Like the paintings on the walls, he looked painfully young.

'In the name of Her Majesty Elizabeth the Third, Queen of Ceylon and of Great Britain, Ireland and the British

Dominions beyond the Seas, Head of the Commonwealth, Defender of the Faiths...'

They stared at him, eyes old and new, dark skins envying the white, a two-thousand year-old civilization broken beneath the glance of this man who looked barely twenty-three, so straight in his scarlet uniform and scraggly mustache.

'We hereby do appoint the House Ratwatte lords of the Ceylonese armed forces, namely the Ceylon Planters Rifle Corps, the Ceylon Defense Force, the Ceylon Light Infantry, and the Ceylon Garrison Artillery...'

And on and on. It was always the same: Ratwatte held the armies, Madugalle – which had more than once sparked a rebellion in the early days – were given the Ministries of Economics and Industry; Rambukpotha got the trade routes and the navy, or what little the British deemed sufficient to protect the Port City nexus that connected the Chinese Silk Road with the British empire. And to the Bandaras, of course, themselves famous provocateurs, went the poorest empire, Reconciliation: on one hand charged with keeping the peace in lands outside of Kandy, on the other hand charged with running the entertainment industry that kept the Ceylonese distracted. Hewage had once called it the most powerful, though, because the Bandaras dealt with fame and image, and with that came the power to shape society and curry favour with all others.

It would always be the same. Every four years the Brits held this as a reminder. We give you power. Remember who you are. You lost. We won. Young, eager men in scarlet dispensed power, and the Inquisition enforced it.

She sighed and went back to thinking about communicators and voice-boxes.

Except this time there was a hush that broke through. She craned her neck.

Three of the House Lords and Ladies were up in front of the British officer, sweating slightly in the heat, looking grand in all their finery.

Only three!

Bandara, Bandara, came a whisper that swept the crowd. The Bandaras had not been announced!

'Well?' said Hewage when he met her in the canteen for their lunch the next day. Like all government offices, the Hub had strict times and places for eating and drinking: stray too far in either direction and you went hungry.

'You first,' she said.

She could feel the glances as they sat down. The whispers. Hundreds of pairs of eyes, flicking towards them with that blatant, almost feral curiosity of the government employee sensing someone with their head on the chopping block.

'Aritha Bandara's been called up before the Inquisition,' he said. 'Disciplinary hearing.'

That was huge. Aritha was Minister of Reconciliation, and as one of the Bandaras, was near untouchable. 'And what happened?'

The old man looked at his rice and curry portions, untouched, and lit a cigarette. She pretended not to notice the slight tremor in his hands.

'They want to know how the hell the bots got up to Kandy, why there weren't safety precautions ... and who to blame for the whole mess. You think a Bandara is going to take the blame? There'll be an Inquiry. They'll find someone lower down the ranks. Maybe in Division Planning. Maybe Transport. Shit flows downhill. Sooner or later, it's going to come down the me.'

'To us.'

He waved the 'us' aside. 'What did you find?'

She related her autopsy: the blocked ports, the disconnected voicebox. He winced.

'Not my design. My boss before me, back when I was your age. I've sent a team out to find and kill any other units like this before anything else happens.'

'I can't diagnose the brain,' she said. 'We'd either need to recast the whole thing with a new neural interface or just boot this one up and try to talk to it.'

'Then talk to it.'

She thought about that empty, childlike face. He saw her wince.

'Go to the workshop,' he said. 'Talk to a guy called Attanayaka in Q.A. Charitha Attanayaka. I'll give him a call. He should be able to hook you up.'

'They'll ask questions,' she said.

'This one won't,' he said. 'He's one of mine.'

'What are you going to do?'

'I'm going to do my best to blame it on some other poor bugger,' he said, his hands shaking very slightly. 'Damned if I'm going to take the blame. Government's all about passing the ball until someone gets caught with it. But I need you to figure out what that bot was doing, why it was here. Either way, get me answers.'

He lit another cigarette. She left him there, smoking and coughing gently, his food still untouched.

FOURTEEN

The ride down to the machine workshop was long and uncomfortable. The elevator, a tiny iron coffin, cranked and creaked and squealed down the many levels. Every so often it would ping open and a guard with an empty black visor would check her pass and nod her onwards. Every so often others would join her, but they were never alone, and never stayed for long. Women in saris and lab coats, men in sarongs and handlebar mustaches.

45

46

47

One last nod, and she was through. A long gray walkway took her to a railing, and suddenly she was there, looking down upon the Machine Workshop.

White concrete, as far as the eye could see, overlaid with glass and steel. Bodies in yellow plastic suits swarmed like ants. The low hum of generators and neon swept over the sounds of industry: the noise of men calling to one another, the tap-tap-tap of metal against metal, the incessant machine whine of 3D printers and drill chisels.

A man waved at her from below. A long flight of stairs led down to him.

He had a long, twitchy face and nervous fingers. 'Almeida?'

She looked at his nametag. 'Attanayaka?'

They shook hands briefly and he led her, coat-tails swishing, past the maze of glass into which they had descended. Down here the glass lines turned into cubicles and rooms. She could not help gawking as they passed. In every cubicle, in various stages of being built, were children.

Here there was a skeleton, clamped and stretched out like a body being racked; a printer head darted over it in precise strokes, laying down muscle fibre that steamed gray in the florescent light. Here there were men in yellow suits putting row upon row of children through their paces; as one they knelt, crouched, spun around, thrust invisible spears. She had spent years seeing these faces live and plunder and loot across projected visions of Colombo, but seeing them here, their innards stripped bare, wires exposed, was unnerving.

'Completely fucked-up, noh?' he asked her as she trailed through these glass visions.

She agreed. Whether it was to the incident or the sight in front of her she didn't quite know.

Finally they came to an office, a small gray concrete thing with the blue lotus and lion crest on the door. He led her in. It was a spartan space, with one wall entirely taken up by a map overlay.

'The old man called me,' he said without preamble. A red ring lit up around the perimeter of the Zone. 'This wasn't supposed to happen. We have hunter units every five hundred meters apart. Nothing mechanical gets in, nothing mechanical gets out.'

'They took one of the supply trains, apparently?'

Three red dots lit up across the train tracks. 'There were those old Conductor units on those trains. Should have stopped them. I say should have, because guess who pulled two of them for some stupid party with the Prime Minister?'

He didn't need to tell her, but if she had three guesses, all three of them would have been Aritha Bandara. The parties at the Bell Tower were notorious: for the guestlists almost as much as the rumors.

'When was this?'

'I don't know, two months ago. Some bullshit excuse. Probably ran out of Chinese hookers and decided to have something else to laugh at this time. We've got the other one in storage here. It looks like it put up a fight, but the kid bots must shorted it out, stuck some water and metal in it. How the hell did bots even think of that?'

She told him what she knew. The girl. The explorer-type. The seals from the machine workshop where the neural link should have been. Even the voicebox. They contemplated the fantastic series of accidents that had led to that terrible moment, and he groaned.

'It'll take me days to recast an interface for that model,' he said. 'I remember the explorer. They used whatever shit was lying around on the desk. No standards, nothing. Best thing I can do right now is give you a new voicebox. Maybe you can talk to it.'

'That's it?'

'It's a black box model, what do you expect?'

'I just want to find out what happened,' she said. 'The old man wants to know how and why she – the bot – made it all the way here, but I'm thinking maybe if we can get a video feed, or a testimonial before the Inquiry, and...'

'And blame Aritha Bandara?'

It did sound remarkably stupid.

'Here's what's going to happen,' he said. 'The old man isn't thinking straight. They're going to ask him why we have prototype explorer bots running around. He's going to think like an engineer and say we need a few testing the bounds, et cetera, et cetera. Or maybe he'll say his old boss sent them out and he had no idea, really. Then they'll ask him why they hadn't been programmed to stop at Colombo. And then it'll come out that we really can't update them. And then they'll ask him who commissioned these. And then all shit hits the fan and everyone in Reconciliation gets held at gunpoint and interrogated and some of us who worked on these things will be dragged out and shot. Aritha won't be within a mile of the hearing.'

'Unless we give them evidence.'

'Unless we give them evidence that doesn't let them pin it on *us*,' he corrected. 'You know he asked me to have a basic bot ready, all smashed up? If you can't crack this one open, I'm to come upstairs and replace yours with a replica.'

He saw her look. 'Yeah. Absolutely normal bot. Nothing out of the ordinary. We scratch our heads and say this was a perfectly normal path and it was that one thing of not having enough protection on the train. That way the only story that can come out is two bots get through the train because someone here in Kandy decided the Conductors should be hauled off as party entertainment. And whoever signed off on that at the bottom end gets shot.'

'Why were they built without interfaces, anyway?' Almeida asked. The question had nagged her ever since the discovery. 'None of this makes sense.'

His nervousness visibly increased, and he lowered his voice. 'I think the old man wanted to create something close to ... well, us,' he said quietly.

'Us?'

'Human. Think about it. No updates, so pre-training, no resets. Just a learning engine that would keep going. He came up with a different neural model, they say. Like a child. Like a real child.'

She was flabbergasted. 'But why?'

'Don't ask me, this was before my time,' he said. 'I'm just telling you what I've heard.'

'But that's ... dangerous. It's not right.'

He gave her a blank look and gestured at the glass cages around us, where thousands of half-built robots were being turned into children by the yellow-suited army.

'I don't know,' he said. 'We're building robots that kill each other for primetime TV. I mean, we sell tour packages where you can go down and kill them yourselves. It's right there on the website. Might as well go the whole hog, eh?'

For a second she wanted to slap him. Well, perhaps not him: just to slap someone, something, for this sudden, insane twist of events that had dumped this in her lap.

They watched the glass cages in silence: children being assembled, children being disassembled.

'You're sure you can't hook me up with an interface?'

'Three days,' he said.

'Fine,' she said. 'Then give me a voicebox, I'll go talk to the damn thing.'

Almeida went home that evening, clutching in her hands the circuit board and the voicebox with the serial numbers filed off. Rain fell from the black sky.

She did not sleep well.

FIFTEEN

The next morning, Almeida found herself looking once more at the corpse of the disassembled girl-bot.

It really was a very small body.

She flipped it over, speaking into the recorder, this time more as a way to distract herself than to keep notes. The voicebox came away in her hand. The new one fitted in quite easily. The neck was a thick bundle of lean plastic wrapped around optical wire and metal wrapped around a rudimentary ball and socket joint; she severed the faux muscles with ease.

'Splenius capitis, semispinalis capitis,' she recited robotically at the recorder, cutting her way through. She found the power cable and followed it up. There was generally a two-ping port here that connected to the stump of the neck. This she connected, with slow, elaborate care, to two wires pulled out of a power supply.

There was a whine, a spark, and the eyes opened. The mouth opened and screamed.

She jumped back. The eyes found her. The scream halted abruptly, like a whistle cut short.

'Hand. Palm turn. Hand. Palm turn,' the mouth said.

It was a toneless voice, neither male nor female.

'Hello,' she said cautiously.

The eyes regarded her warily. Then they looked down to the scalpel in her hand.

'Hand. Point. Hand. Palm. Turn.'

Of course. The voicebox. The previous one had been configured for gestures: had those commands, used over and over again, ingrained themselves in the brain? She approached cautiously, scalpel clutched tight, and looked over the head, trying to ignore the hideously lifelike eyes that tracked her out of that child's face.

There were commands flowing to nonexistent neck muscles: she could see the sparks at the ends of filaments, winking in and out. The head tried to turn. She saw first surprise, then alarm.

'Point! Point!' the head screamed.

She pulled the plug. And, shaking, she reconnected the old voicebox and scrolled through the list of commands. Whatever the bot was saying, it had to be in here.

The lines of text scrolled on the screen. Here it was: a series of motion models linked to statement lists. She browsed through the keywords.

Hand. Palm. Turn. Generic question. *What happened?*

Point. Point. Imperative. *Stay away.*

The bot was terrified.

She called Attanayake.

'I've found an archive of old opcodes,' Attanayake said. 'Try these.'

Almeida spoke the opcodes Attanayaka had given her. The panic vanished from the bot's eyes, replaced by something gentler and more curious. There. It was in safe mode now, all defensive protocols turned off.

'I'm not going to hurt you,' she said, speaking low and calm without even meaning to: babyvoice. 'You're hurt. I'm a doctor.'

The head blinked, tensor connections sparking furiously.

'Reference: cassette 1131,' it said, and looked surprised at itself. 'Point-self? Ears? Speak? Speak?'

That was progress. She dived for the communications list again. Cassette 1131. No audio saved, of course – if only she would be so lucky; but a set of keywords: *inquiry, location, health, general.*

The rest she could guess.

'You're fine,' she said gently. 'You won't be able to feel your body. You're hurt. I'm trying to fix you.'

It listened to her intently.

'Speak? Speak?'

'You can speak now,' she said, and found herself smiling involuntarily. She stopped the moment she realized.

'Can speak,' the head said, and even to her ears it sounded astonished. 'Can speak!'

And now came the part she dreaded. 'I'm going to leave you here for a bit,' she said slowly, backing away. 'It's going to take some time for your to learn how to talk, so you're going to need to be awake. I'll be back, okay?'

'Can speak,' said the head slowly, as if savouring the words. It saw her edging away. The little-girl eyebrows rose. 'Can speak. Point-self. Point-you. Go. Don't. Go. Don't...'

She slipped out of the door and shut it behind her. Dammit, it didn't look real, but it sounded it.

'Day one,' she said into her recorder. 'Voicebox integration initiated.'

She reported this to Hewage, who mulled over it and picked up the phone. He barked something into it.

'How long until you get the interface?' he asked her.

'Attanayaka says a couple more days.'

He harumph'd. 'And the voicebox?'

'Might take a day to set, apparently. What do we do until then?'

'We're government employees, we do what government employees do,' he said. 'Eat the lunch, drink the tea, pass the ball.'

≈

The next day she walked in to the sound of someone humming.

It was the head. The little girl-bot had closed her eyes and was humming – or singing: whatever it was, it was beautiful, for the voicebox, unfettered by human restraints, replicated the sound of violins perfectly. Had Almeida grown up in Colombo, she would have recognized Max Bruch's first violin concerto, known sometimes as the Music that Did Not Kill.

Suddenly the little head paused. 'THE BLUETOOTH DEVICE IS READY TO PAIR,' it screamed in an awful pseudo-Chinese accent, and fell silent. The eyes caught sight of Two and tracked her, alert, but no longer scared.

'Hello.'

'Hello,' said the head.

'Can you understand me?'

'Can you understand me?'

She brought up her recorder. 'Day two. Subject appears to be mimicking sound patterns.'

'Day two,' said the head. 'Subject appears to be mimicking sound patterns.'

The eyes stared at her, unafraid, curious.

She sighed, ignoring the echo from the head, and looked around the office. It was a large space, but this bot business was clearly not doing it any favours: it was littered with tools and discarded meal wrappers.

Almeida set to cleaning it, keeping an eye on the bot. An hour or so passed, represented mostly by several empty packets of noodles and a can of beer.

'Hands. Legs. No,' the head said suddenly.

She drew close to it.

'Hands. Legs. No,' the girl-bot repeated, eyes darting at the ground. 'The Bluetooth device is ready to pair.'

She understood, or thought she did. 'Yes, your hands and legs are gone.'

'Dead?'

Well, there was no use lying. 'Dead.'

There was a pause. 'See. Sky,' it said. 'See. Sky. Sky. Clouds. Sky.'

And it went on repeating that: See. Sky. Clouds. Sky. It was awful how repetitive a voice could get when delivered at the exact same tone and frequency. She eventually figured it out and rotated it to where it could see a screen, and on the screen she ran a loop of the sky outside.

'Sky,' it said once, and smiled. 'Boy? Food?'

Boy? She flipped through the autopsy report. The other bot. A boy. This one was a nasty piece of work. Long limbs, slightly disjointed, splayed; something about it reminded her of an animal. The video footage was brutal; it dodged, screamed, was shot.

She showed this to the head. The reaction was immediate: the girl-bot began to wail.

Almeida grabbed the recorder, stunned. 'Subject was exposed to video footage of the destruction of its companion unit,' she said into the small metal grille. She looked at the scrunched up eyes, the face set in a scream. 'I don't know what's happening, but I think it's crying.'

≈

'Are they supposed to do that?' she asked Hewage that evening. She showed him the footage. He watched, an unlit cigarette dangling from his lip, hair grayer than ever.

'It's not the first one I've seen cry,' he said. He didn't take his eyes off the screen, though. 'We've had a handful before, in whom crying evolved as some sort of pain response. Usually happens in loners. Some sort of soft reset.'

'What does it mean?'

'Doesn't mean anything,' he said. 'It's just a black box, Almeida. Input, output. Somewhere along the line some three-bit emotion simulator figured out how to cry and there was no feedback to short out that output. You've seen the Zone. They're interesting, but these things have as much meaning as my cigarette.'

He handed her recorder back. 'This thing looks like it's going to take bloody ages to interrogate.'

'Attanayaka should be done with the interface soon,' she said. 'I'll be able to look at the video feed directly then.'

He nodded.

'What's happening with the Inquiry?'

'Coming closer,' he said. 'Everyone knows it now. I got a call from the Police Commissioner yesterday. One of the men killed, his family apparently refused the bribe, took it to Court. Some fool officer took their statement. Now the Houses can't hush it up anymore.'

'What'll they do?'

'If it turns out to be defective bots, Aritha will make some idiot down at the machine workshop explain how they took a spear to the head or something and went a bit crazy. He'll fire someone to make things look right. If it's an issue of security, Aritha's in trouble. He can pass it down to whoever handles the trains, and they'll say Aritha took the conductors, and maybe the Bandaras get trampled into the mud a bit. Good for us. But if it turns out this bot was different from the start, that its software...' he fumbled for a lighter and lit his cigarette, and took a long drag. 'Well, Aritha passes it on to me, and I can't pass it back. They'll give me pension and send me out to the Zone for life. My kid's going to grow up without a father.'

It was funny, how she'd worked with him for years, but only now saw the droop in his spine, the bags under his eyes. She had, she realized with a tinge of surprise, never questioned: never asked him why he did what he did, or even where he came from, or where he disappeared to when their shift was done.

'You have a family?' she asked.

'Wife,' he said. 'A kid. We're behind on the school fees.' He gestured with the cigarette. 'We live over there. Rent sucks.'

'Maybe they'll cut you some slack. Not exactly your fault, right?'

'Not how it works,' he said quietly. 'Government employees, remember. People say jump, we ask how high. People say off with their heads, we stick our heads down and our asses out. Maybe the guy before me died for someone else's stupidity, and maybe this is all part of the job.'

He looked up at the empty, gray sky. 'It was good money,' he said, almost to himself.

That evening she retraced her steps down the slow roads of Kandy, her plastic coat wrapped tightly against the soft drizzle.

The road led her down from the Ministry Hub towards the city center, taking her past a world of mostly empty hills and stunted trees. Very few people came this way – even the occasional tourist heading to or from the hotels would think twice about crossing all the way here, close as it was to the city center. It was just her and the Hub and the open road and that billboard for the Wars...

The billboard. It hung in tatters, strips streaming in the half-wind. Pasted crudely over what remained were two large, clear photos of the girl-bot and the boy-bot. Right from the final moments. They hung there wearing ten-foot expressions of fear and surprise. Angry bloodlike strokes screamed 'EPA!' across their faces.

She shivered and moved on. Someone would see that, and she didn't want to be around when they did.

SIXTEEN

The next day, one of Attanayaka's boys – twice as twitchy as his superior – showed up at her office clutching a parcel. It turned out to be a small gray thing with all sorts of protrusions and a complex wiring schematic.

'Shutdown,' Almeida told the head, which had been watching her in silence.

The eyelids drooped. She unhooked the thing and began the laborious process of welding the new interface into the shunt. Eventually it was ready; she plugged in her computer, kicked the chair away and started typing. The filesystem mounted, the clustered drives within the head yielding up their secrets one by one.

/root/inputarchive
/root/preprocess
/root/mainmodel
/root/learning

≈

It was slightly different from what she was used to, but she recognized the structure. Logs of input data from the eyes and ears. Preprocessing math that would convert the input into a data matrix that the personality could process. Code for learning that would kick in at night, assimilating lessons learnt and feeding them back into the main model.

Out of curiosity, she tried the mainmodel and learning folders. The personality files, as expected, were unreadable. The learning code was strange: it referenced all sorts of variables she'd never heard of and seemed to be set to run all the time. Either way, nothing useful there.

/inputarchive

And here was the video, categorized neatly by folders. She scrolled through the endless sea of folders, awe-struck by the amount of data.

A logfile lay at the end of the folder.

At some point it had started running out of space and started deleting old memories. Here was an equally endless list of dates forgotten, memories wiped in a flash, with only the lessons remaining in the gibberish matrix of the personality.

One folder for each day of the bot's life. This thing had been running for twenty years.

She called Hewage. 'I'm in.'

He sounded terse. 'Last six months of data. Copy it, and wipe the bot.'

'Why?'

'There's a time for questions, but it isn't now,' he said sharply. 'Just do what I say. Attanayake will be up there in an hour.'

'Is this the Inquiry?'

The line went dead.

An hour later, when Attanayaka knocked on her door with a heavy cloth bundle in his arms, she knew. They unwrapped the bundle, careful not to meet each other's eyes, and there on the table was an almost exact replica of the girl-bot that had died in Kandy; bullet holes, scuff marks included. The part of the head that held the drives was smashed beyond repair.

They packed the ruins of the original bot, numbering anything she had removed as they went.

'Power supply.'

'Left shoulder motor.'

'Back muscles. Put them in the bag.'

Everything seemed so small now. He gestured to her for the head, still connected to her computer.

'I – we might need that,' she said.

'No evidence,' he said.

She unhooked the head, moving gently, and on impulse wrapped it up in a piece of cloth before giving it to him. Somehow it seemed wrong to look at those eyes.

'When they come and ask you, tell them you couldn't extract any data, and hand the body over,' he said. 'They'll send it down to me for verification. I sign off. We never talk about this again.'

'Is that what Hewage said?'

Attanayaka gave her that blank look of his. 'I owe the man my job,' he said, and vanished, leaving her with a fresh corpse on the table.

Almeida moved with the urgency of panic. From the recorder logs she extracted the notes of the autopsy and put them into a report. After a brief moment of thought, she took out the scalpel again and made new, deeper cuts elsewhere: along the power lines, the skeleton core, the input nodes. Bit by bit the child's face fell away and she was left holding a metal carcass; then she stapled it all back together. There. Now it looked like as thorough an autopsy as could be.

To her report she added a note about how the memory modules were damaged but the body seemed otherwise perfectly normal.

And she waited in her gray cube of an office.

They came in a tide of black robes and shaved heads. Very polite. They kept their guns pointed away from her. Attanayaka was summoned and the corpse handed over to his care; he managed a wink as they led him away. She was led, trailing whispers, to an unmarked white van that waited outside.

Soon, she found herself in a house. It was small, but very carefully built; the roof, a great inverted cone, curled into a staircase that plunged into an open hall and a courtyard, turning rain into a slim waterfall.

There was nothing around for miles; only the steep slope of the hill and scrub. A mist hung about the whole place.

They led her to a glass wall overlooking the lake from afar. A pale man sat in front of a table; angular, bespectacled, dressed in the Western style – a suit, a shirt, boots. Few dared dress like that.

He wore gloves.

She felt a hard core of fear rise in her and fought to swallow it.

'You know who I am?' the man said. Polished, perfect British English, none of the usual Ceylonese cadences.

'Yes, sir.'

The two Inquisitor-monks who had led her here bowed to the man and vanished.

The Chief Inquisitor of Kandy gestured for her to take a seat. 'Tea?'

'I. Er. Yes, thank you,' she stammered.

He placed a cup in front of her – fine porcelain, carved with the lily and the lion. A teapot next. Something about how he moved struck her as not altogether human; the movements were too precise, too measured, like a fine piece of clockwork put into motion, a stark contrast from the irregularities of flesh.

She watched, mesmerized with both fear and awe. The tea was poured. It was hot and fresh; she sipped cautiously and tried to hide the slight shaking of her fingers.

'Almeida? Of the estate Almeidas?'

'Yes, sir.'

Soft brown eyes watched her. 'You know your grandfather was a monk right here in the Inquisition,' he said. 'Your family is very well known to us.'

Again, that way of speaking: neither a question, nor a statement, but this time with a definite hint of something else.

'I'm told you worked on the autopsy of the robot that broke into our city the other day.'

'Yes, sir.'

'Tell me what you know.'

She recited what she knew, almost from memory. The break-in at the station. The death toll. The Mahanayake, the head monk, calling for the punishment of all responsible.

The mob that lined the streets and smashed the police wagon carrying the bodies, ripping apart the boy-bot in a frenzy.

She started to tell him that the girl bot was perfectly normal, that this was likely the fault of poor security along the train line. Not to mention the Conductors, or to lay blame on anyone, just enough to push the ball out of their department...

And she couldn't. Those soft brown eyes fixed on hers with unyielding scrutiny. And it spilled out; the welded seals, the explorer model, the singing, the grief, the feeling that this thing was, somehow, more alive than the others they'd seen.

'They always tell the truth,' he said to himself. 'Why torture people when you can give them tea instead, eh? So. Who replaced the body? Hewage?'

'And Attanayaka,' she found herself saying, panic-stricken. 'They said if ... if the Inquiry found out, we'd be blamed for having those bots running around...'

He smiled. It was not a reassuring smile. 'And here the Inquiry *has* found out,' he said.

Tears welled in her eyes. 'It's not our fault.'

He pursed his lips. 'Viewed from above, this whole scenario is like a clock with many damaged parts,' he said. 'Isolated failures that, in the normal order of things, would have been glossed over, but in tandem caused catastrophic failure in the entire system.'

'Yes, sir.'

'One cannot expect a mob to take that view.'

'Yes, sir.'

'Our job is take that view and to prevent a witchhunt. To make sure justice is served logically and that only the right necks hang.'

'Yes, sir.'

'If you lie to me again, or I find you are holding back something, or protecting someone... your neck, and your family's necks, will join those guilty in the noose.'

She gulped. 'Yes, sir.'

'Good,' he said. 'Good, good.'

'Sir?' she ventured. 'What – what happens now?'

'Nothing,' he said. 'I've asked you questions, you've answered honestly. You will be called when it is time for your testimony. When that time comes, I want you to go up there and tell them that it was a perfectly normal bot, and that its memory was damaged beyond repair. Until that time, you will stay at home, you will not contact anyone outside your immediate family, and you will be monitored. Understood?'

'Sir? You want me to – lie?'

'It shouldn't be too hard,' he said. 'The drugs will have worn off by then.'

He held a hand out for the teacup.

SEVENTEEN

The Court summons came three days later. She knew it was coming: Hewage hadn't come to work for two days, the gossip around the canteen had doubled, and everyone seemed to know she'd been working on the autopsy. Even her mother started asking about her work: the kind of small talk that led to lowered voices and hard questions. They wanted to know about Hewage. Had he orchestrated the whole thing? Was it true that he had a grudge against the Bandaras?

'This way, Miss Almeida,' said the nondescript policeman they sent to pick her up. Besides him was a monk of the Inquisition.

The police wagon took them down the slow roads and into the traffic. Red lights glared at them the whole way.

'Traffic, bung,' came a voice from the front.

The policeman who sat with her frowned. 'Everybody's heading to the courts,' he said.

From every car, from every van and bus and door, flags waved. The betel leaf. The elephant. The colors of the Great Houses peppered the traffic; here a Bandara supporter, there a Aditya, there someone pledged to the sprawling merchant-family of the Hettiges. Those on the pavements wore their colors less defiantly, but no less openly; under clear plastic coats were green and red shirts, black skirts, sharp divisions. The policeman saw her gaze and cursed.

'Bad to put a Bandara on trial,' he said.

The dull gray statues of monks in front of the high court seemed to beckon them onward. The wagon turned on its lights and went to join the cordon.

The rest of it passed by in a daze. There was a huge roar. Noise. She remembered policemen linking their arms around her; the bright flashes of the photographers, outshining the sun like a thousand popping stars; the Inquisition monk slowly parting a way through the crowd; the wooden doors rolling open solemnly. The courtroom was packed wall to wall and deathly silent. Projected on one side of the wall was the reason they were here: the bullet-riddled bodies of the two bots – and assorted photos of the carnage they had caused. Men screaming, cut in half. A woman with her hands chopped off. A child speared through.

'Next witness, Dr Kushlani de Almeida,' called the Mahanayake's voice, rolling over the assembly like water off a duck.

It hit her hard. A hint of darkness began to crowd the edges of her vision. Moving on jellylike knees she ascended the witness stand.

'Please state your occupation.'

'Second Assistant Overseer at the Ministry of Reconciliation.'

'And what do you do?'

She explained the job, feeling a little more comfortable. Overseeing. Making sure the broadcasts were set up right and the wars happened the way they should and the numbers stacked up right. She realized, midway through her explanation, that she was describing...

'So would we be right in assuming you helped orchestrate and oversee the blood sports and the bots, Miss Almeida?'

Yes. She helped orchestrate wars for a sixty-thousand-rupee salary.

'Part of your job involves diagnostics and repair, does it not?'

'I rarely directly repair things, but diagnostics, yes,' she said. 'If something goes wrong, we're supposed to examine the unit, figure out what happened, and submit a bug report to the machine workshop so they can fix it.'

The lawyer, opulent in her rich sari, looked satisfied. She went on. Did Almeida receive the infamous killer bot for diagnosis?

Yes.

Was there anything odd about the unit in question?

Aside from extensive damage, no.

The unit was operating as normal, within normal parameters?

A sweat broke out on her forehead. She half expected the Chief Inquisitor to appear and declare her a liar. But nothing happened; nobody moved. No Inquisitors were amongst the audience.

'Yes,' she lied. 'To the best of my knowledge, it was a normal bot.'

'And this incident could have happened with any other unit?'

'I assume so.'

'In your opinion, what could have led to the breakout that happened?'

She caught sight of Hewage in the audience. He nodded almost imperceptibly. 'I don't know,' she said, trying not to make it look like she was going to blame someone. 'We have extensive security along the perimeter to make sure this doesn't happen. Under normal circumstances they would have been destroyed once they got to the train.'

'By?'

'The Conductor units, of course.'

'How many Conductor units are there?'

'Three.'

There was a collective aaah from the audience. A picture flicked up on the wall. It was a blurry selfie, taken at night. Aritha Bandara's handsome, slightly drunk-looking face took up most of the foreground. But but there was no mistaking the leering bulk of a Conductor in the back; it stood in the middle of a crowd of scantily dressed people; it was dressed in what looked like silks and was carrying what looked like a couple of plates.

'This was taken from Mister Bandara's social media,' said the lawyer. 'Do you recognize that bot in the background?'

It was cut and dried and easy now. 'That's one of the Conductor bots,' she said.

'Thank you. No further questions, hamudhuruwane,' said the lawyer, looking up to where the Budhhist high priest, the Mahanayake, sat in judgement. The lawyer had the look of someone who knew, very clearly, that she was winning by a long mile.

≈

They called up Attanayaka and Hewage next. The case was ironclad by the time Attanayaka was done; Hewage laid the nail in the coffin. There was a low, angry buzzing among the audience. The jury of House Peers looked very much like an argument ready to explode. Only the Mahanayake, in his saffron robes, looked unfazed.

She sneaked a look at Aritha Bandara, sober and pale, sitting there in his sarong with his family colors on his shirt. One by one, the family members at his side withdrew. By the time the jury broke, he was sitting alone, thin-lipped, his expression the panicked fury of a man drowning.

Hewage was outside. Hanging on to his leg, like a spider, was a child; trailing a little distance away, looking both relieved and angry at the same time, was his wife. He was trying to light a cigarette. The wife exclaimed angrily and slapped it out of his mouth. He looked rueful, and excused himself and walked over to Two.

'Good job,' he said.

'They know,' she said. 'The Inq...'

The fear must have been evident on her face. 'I don't think anything will happen to us,' he said guardedly. 'We're in the public eye for now, it won't do to make us disappear. Ball's in someone else's court now. We just need to know what the game is.'

They looked out at the crowd, who looked back: a waving sea of House colors. The Bandaras were breaking away in twos and threes; the police stood by anxiously.

'Appachchi, appachchi,' said the child, tugging at his trouser.

He looked down, and for a moment a smile drew a crease across his tired face.

'Let's go eat something,' he said, lifting up the child. 'Come on. Let's get out of here.'

EIGHTEEN

It was many weeks before the Ministry got back to something resembling its normal form. Nobody had believed Aritha Bandara could ever be carted away, but there he was, sentenced to life in prison: in the true manner of Sri Lankan politicians, he would spend most of that time feigning illness in a special ward in the prison hospital; but something had been done.

The Inquisitors was terribly efficient. They first came for those who had been known favourites, those undue appointments, and they were soon earmarked for transfers far, far away: possibly to the thorium factories in the North-East. A new Minister was appointed with all speed – a nervous, twitching man, who reminded them all too much of Attanayake; he gave a brief speech and was never heard from again.

Then came the shakedown visits. Gray surplus corridors were filled with unsmiling monks with guns on one side, and terrified Ministry employees on the other. One by one the names were called.

'Hewage, Anton.'

The corridor of nervous titters hushed. Hewage, pale despite himself, took one last puff, ground his cigarette into the floor, and went in.

'Kushlani de Almeida.'

She adjusted her sari and walked in. Curiously, she felt light, as if the courtroom had taken all her fear away.

Inside was an old office – a dark, shabby thing with two three Inquisitors in it. One, a giant of a man with a pudgy face and gold-rimmed spectacles, sat at a desk. He grinned owlishly at them when they entered.

'Do sit,' he said, the clipped British accent turning it into an order.

They sat with a nervous squeak of chairs and tried not to look at each other.

'Tea? Biscuits?'

Both appeared before either of them could reply. The pudgy Inquisitor clapped his hands.

'Now we just need to wait for ten minutes, to make it look official,' he said, dipping his biscuit into his tea. He leaned over the desk like a co-conspirator. Servomotors whined in his shoulders and somewhere from his back. Almeida fought the urge to lean back: the man was a giant, and he seemed to bend almost the length of the desk.

'Thanks to you two and your genius scrambling, we managed to get Aritha Bandara behind bars. That's the balance of power in this city sorted for the next fifty years! By the way, we need to make sure nobody knows what you've done. Perhaps we can give you a slap? Or imprison one of your children for a week or something?'

They both hastened to assure him that a slap was not needed.

There was a soft *plunk* from the teacup, and the Inquisitor's face fell. The soggy biscuit had fallen in.

'Oh,' he said unhappily. 'The Bandaras are like this biscuit, you know. Actually, all these families are. Every so often they soak up too much power and someone breaks off and does something stupid.'

Somehow the sight of an Inquisitor explaining politics with a soggy biscuit was too much.

'So. Let's get on with it, then. Hewage. You're up for Undersecretary to the new Minister in six months. It'll probably be another Bandara and given how good you are at rolling balls out of your court you'll fit right it. We need you to be our eyes and ears at the highest level.'

'I'm happy where I am, sir,' said Hewage.

'You don't have a choice. I'm told you either take the job or we shoot you for obstruction of justice or something like that. Besides, it's a better paycheck and you get Ministry quarters. Nice apartments. I've been there.'

'Yes, sir.'

'Almeida, you get a promotion, small pay rise, more tea coupons at the canteen. We expect you to be ready to take over Hewage's job as Controller when he leaves. Chief sends his regards.'

Despite the situation, Almeida fought back the urge to punch the air. Six months ago she'd been faced with the prospect of waiting until Hewage died before she'd ever get to the Controller position.

'Don't speak a word about this for the next six months. We'll spend some more time here, make it look like I'm really making you suffer, and then you go back to your lives. When things are ready, they'll happen.'

Hewage, no doubt guessing what she was thinking, shot her a look.

'What do we do now, sir?' he asked.

'Up to you, really,' said the Inquisitor. 'You could read a book. Ten minutes is a long time.'

≈

And eventually life at the Ministry of Reconciliation went back to normal: an endless display of 10'o clock meetings and arguments over tea coupons and needless overtime.

And Almeida found herself poring over those videos that she'd never been able to look at. The last six months of Silent girl's life.

It was . ..if she had to use a word, it would have been 'fascinating'. But it was also perverse, in a sense, watching someone's life unfold, even if it wasn't a life as such.

Here she was, standing in a long queue under the hot sun, one more body in a line of browned bodies, bits of metal poking out here and there where the skin had cracked and failed. They waited for the Chinese to give them their food. The 'milk' which was not milk, but lubricant synthesized from algae; the 'biscuits', the little hard pellets of energy that the little bodies burned.

She saw the Chinese lady smile and give this one more than the usual share.

She saw the long trudge back to the ruined hotel in Colombo-3, the panic of fending off leaner, hungrier bots. The ones that the lines rejected. They crawled and snarled, sensors destroyed beyond belief, their chrome showing, and she saw how terrified the little girl-bot was of them; how the spear stabbed with unfailing precision, puncturing a heart-battery here, a control cord there.

She saw the sunset, and watched it through Silent girl's eyes, and saw the loneliness of waiting for the next one.

And here were rituals. The Sons of Cinnamon Grand. The Children of the Taj. Some fool from marketing had thought those up; bots tethered to popular old sites, given implicit instructions to set up little kingdoms of their own in the corpses of the old hotels.

Initially they'd fought each other fiercely whenever they met – that was the idea; great for generating snapshots for primetime trailers. This was back in the days when the test zone was the biggest show. But the encounters had been too random, the individual bots too short-lived; ratings had dropped, and the Ministry put together a new zone, a replica of the old Colombo Fort area, and thus brought in the recurring narrative of the Fort versus the old Trace City. People liked that. There was a story, albeit enforced largely by Ministry employees sent to Fort on hazard pay.

So they had moved out, and struck a deal with the Chinese Port City to keep the bots fed. They were still useful for trailers and things of that nature. The Fort itself was too carefully balanced for camera crews to go in there and shoot trailer footage. Everyone naturally assumed the tribes would kill each other off.

But they didn't. Through the eyes of this girl-bot, this Silent girl, she saw something different. She saw bots from the two groups meet and hail each other, and share food; she saw patrols, and nods, and lines beyond which they did not step; and once she saw the council where everyone gathered on neutral turf and spoke. She didn't quite understand the language, but the concept translator program picked up the Sinhala-Tamil mix. Food. Water. Ways to avoid the guns of the American Embassy.

Dying friends.

Partnerships. Water from Colombo-3. Metalworks from Colombo-4.

Improvization. Adaptation. Survival.

And this bot, this Silent girl, always there, always surviving.

'It's impressive,' she confided to Hewage over lunch. 'The level of self-organization ... our bot seems to have worked with everyone. That was odd. Like they respected her.'

'Bots don't have the concept of respect,' said Hewage flatly. 'They can't. It's utility or nothing.'

'Kind of like a lot of people I know,' she offered.

Hewage grunted, amused.

'I told the wife about the promotion,' he said.

'You weren't supposed to.'

'Things haven't been easy for her these past few years,' he said. 'Thought she could use a bit of hope.'

'And was she? Hopeful?'

'Now she's nagging me about having new shirts made,' he said with a half-smile. 'Dress for my new station, whatnot. I keep telling her I'd rather have a full stomach than a linen shirt.'

≈

Almeida didn't return to her desk that evening, but instead punched out a half-day. She needed to be out of the Hub. Hewage was clearly coming to relish the thought of his new role. The lunchtime canteen chatter was slowly moving on from the trial and the debauchery of Aritha Bandaranaike to who-said-who and who-married-whom. There was that slow, oppressive sense of a machine righting itself.

Not for the first time, she found herself thinking that the humans she worked with were not all that different from the machine societies they built. Something would topple, something would change, but eventually the whole thing would reset, and it would be as if none of this ever happened.

She thought of going home, but then home, too, was stasis of a different kind. Instead she walked and walked under the gray skies until she came to a bridge and hailed a passing taxi. It took her to a hotel that overlooked the lake at the heart of. There was a rooftop bar that looked out at the dreary trees that orbited it, and the golden roof of the temple. It was quiet here.

The waist-jacketed and sarong'd waiter floated by and gave her her Long Island iced tea: a blasphemy to both the island and tea, no doubt, but a large amount of alcohol in a glass was still a large amount of alcohol in a glass. She sipped it slowly, thinking.

'Pardon me,' said a sonorous at her elbow. 'You're the girl from the Aritha Bandara case?'

She turned. There was an older man behind her, large, round of belly, dressed in what she thought of as old cricket club attire: a crisp white shirt, a blazer that looked like it had seen better days, jeans. A press pass dangled from his neck.

'No comments,' she said automatically.

The man smiled, palms open. He had an open sort of face, generic and double-chinned. 'Please, no reporting, Miss de Almeida. Even us old journalists must go off duty, noh? May I join you for a drink?'

Well, she didn't want to be too rude. She assented, and the man puffed his way onto a chair next to her, carefully placing a battered laptop bag and a camera on the table. He snapped his fingers and ordered arrack, and with a brief inquiry at her, roasted cashewnuts and pork. The staple of Ceylonese drinking.

Slightly mollified, she responded to his idle chit-chat. The case, obviously. Nothing she hadn't heard before, but 'a Bandara being put away is huge, nah? Those buggers have been in power since the 1990's!' to the plans to resurrect the old Cricket World Cup 'You think Pakistan will send a team this time? Madness. Plague took their best players, now all they're good for is the under-sixteens, nah,' to the always-welcome 'Would you like another drink? I am not a rich man, but we got paid today.'

'Yes, please,' she said gingerly, handing her glass to the waiter, who reappeared with a fresh tower of alcohol.

After a while, she asked him about his job, and nodded slowly through the long-winded explanations. She had wanted to be a journalist, once, before her father took her aside and explained that it was no way for a respectable woman to make a living.

'You see, most of my job is talking to people and going to lunches and things and hoping there's either arrack or a story,' he said, a little unhappily. 'But what about you? Tell me about your job at the Ministry?'

'Second Assistant Zone Controller,' she said, a little proudly, and almost added *soon to be Zone Controller.*

'Not married?'

She frowned. 'No.'

He nodded, as if that explained many things.

'So you handle all the Blood Sports, is it...'

'Well, we make sure the Zone's set up and running properly,' she explained. 'Cameras, livestreams, are there enough bots on both sides for a war, are there any other factors, so on. Like once we had a bit of a flood situation and the side that was most likely going to lose ended up dumping electric cables in the water and destroying half the other side in seconds. Things happen.'

'Hmm,' he said, swilling his drink. There was silence for a while. 'You know, maybe I'm an old man, but I never got into watching the Sport. Something about those children, noh? Like they're alive, somehow.'

'Realism's the selling point, isn't it?'

'Ah. Yes. Realism. But tell me, do they actually feel pain? Because that would be horrible, nah. Because it looks like they feel, nah? Are they like us? Do they do things we do?'

'Well,' she began, and stopped herself. Silent girl was a different thing. 'Chinese rooms. Do you know the argument?'

'Beg pardon?'

How to explain this to someone outside the field? 'So there was a scientist called Searle back in 1980,' she said. 'He said, imagine you're an English speaker locked in a room. Nobody knows who you are. Imagine you have some Chinese text, like a library of Chinese books with phrases in them, and a set of rules in English that tell you what phrases to pick in response to other phrases. Like if someone gives you a set of Chinese characters, you know which book to pick and which page to flip to and which answer to give in return.'

'Like how my son learned Chinese. Locked the bugger in his room until he passed his exams. Okay.'

She winced a bit at the mental image. 'Now imagine a whole bunch of people are outside the room and they keep sending you letters in Chinese. Slipping them under the door. You don't know what they say, but the library and your rules let you pick responses for sentence in every letter they send. And the library is so good that everyone outside think you're a native Chinese speaker, because you're giving the right answers.'

'Okay.'

'But you don't speak Chinese.'

'Nah?'

'No. You just appear to speak Chinese. You have your rules and your library. It looks like you know the language, but you're really thinking in English, and you have no idea what you're saying in Chinese. And that's how the bots work, right. They're Chinese rooms. They have their rulesets, they have their libraries, and the responses appear to be as humanlike as possible...'

'But they're not really understanding, just picking answers from a script?'

'Exactly!' she felt elation at having explained it to a Normal, and clinked her glass with his, feeling pleasantly high from the alcohol. She could see him turning it over in his mind.

'But the thing is,' he said slowly. 'If I'm an English speaker in this room, and I do this often enough, with the rules and the text and what not ... bear with me here ... I'd actually end up learning Chinese?'

She started to deny it, but the image of Silent girl flashed in her mind.

'I mean, if I memorize those rules eventually? Back to my son, that's how he learned. That's how we all learn, nah? I went to school and some biddy showed me the letters and they did this for years until I could have a conversation.'

A bot with its learning engine perpetually turned on, a bot that couldn't be updated or reset...

'Hello, Miss?' he said, peering at her. 'Earth to Miss de Almeida.'

She snapped back and forced a smile. 'Sorry, just thinking. For humans, yes. Bots just don't have that kind of learning mechanism.'

But they do.

He nodded, arrack-drunk. 'Puppets, the lot of them,' he said, slurring very slightly, and downed his glass. 'How are you getting home'

She glanced outside. It was evening; the sun was about to set. The gray-green landscape lit up in a haze of gold.

'I'll take a cab later,' she said, still thinking about the Chinese room.

'You know, I can drop you,' he said. 'I live just nearby...'

She was drunk, but not enough to miss the implication. She looked at him: this old man with his tales of his son and his love of cricket, his preppy white shirt unbuttoned slightly, with his open, pleasant face now in a half-hopeful, half-tipsy smirk, and felt disgusted. For once she had thought it was conversation, just conversation between two strangers in a bar, and nothing else. Why were men like this?

'I'll see myself home, thanks,' she said.

'No trouble, young ladies shouldn't have to go alone...'

'Go home,' she commanded.

The spell broke. The hopeful smirk vanished, replaced by shame and resentment. 'Well, nice meeting you, Miss Almeida,' he said, trying for a hearty brush-off. 'I shall be on my way then.'

She let him have that. He collected his things and weaved gently out of the room. She turned back to her drink and her sunset, thinking of Chinese rooms and bots who couldn't be reset.

NINETEEN

The next day she went back to office. Assistant One had returned, having conveniently missed all of the drama, and Hewage had left instructions to give him as much work as possible and make him suffer. One bristled at the seemingly sudden switch in their ranks, but one call from Hewage sent him scuttling back to his desk.

There. Done.

She blocked out a chunk of time on her calendar and thought about those videos. It was a tremendous amount of data: she'd need a faster way to go through it. They had a program that could parse video frame by frame and report basic statistics on what was in it: like the English speaker in the Chinese room, it had been trained to detect objects. She fired it up and ran the first video through it:

Runtime: 1 hour 12 minutes

Objects detected: Humans, 3, buildings, 22, vehicles, none

It was the work of a minute to write a script that would feed every video into this. Basic programming. She let it run and went for lunch.

The reports were ready by the time she got back. The first three months were very uniform. Lots of alone time. Lots of buildings. Funny that the program kept pegging the bots as humans, it was really starting to get into her head now. Whatever humans appeared were wild scavengers: she saw bleak metal skulls roaming the rooftops, their cries and screams, issued from warped voiceboxes, truly hideous to hear. She watched one or two, feeling the fear as Silent girl ran from them, and, if ambushed, fought back in a whirl of panic and deadly improvised spears.

She shuddered.

The next three months were different. There was always one bot in the frame most of the time.

The boy.

She watched, intrigued, as if she was right there.

A video here. The boy across from her. She extended a hand and offered him some of that ghastly food they ate, keeping a spear-tip pointed at his throat.

He accepted, moving with a curiously neurotic mix of friendliness and fear.

She could feel the caution, the terror on both sides.

A week later. An empty, broken landscape: roads torn up, the shells of prop vehicles so badly degraded that not even the program could pick them up. A sunset; gold across a beautiful blue sky, the likes of which Kandy would never see. And, in the distance, that rotting mountain of refuse and garbage that they had dumped in Colombo.

A noise behind her. Footsteps. Two, watching, jumped. On the screen, Silent girl whirled around, ready to kill.

It was the boy. Palms open. That universal gesture for friendliness. The spear was relaxed. The boy joined her to look at the sunset. Two found herself smiling in relief, her heart still in her throat.

What a life these bots lead, she thought...

Wait.

Were the bots just staring at the sunset?

She watched that entire video. They were. The boy linked hands with the girl and they stared at the sunset.

They weren't supposed to do that.

She watched it again, and again, and again.

Beauty. They were mesmerized by the sunset. Nowhere in the training program was that supposed to be an output.

She had a little paper notebook that she had bought: expensive, but paper couldn't be hacked or accessed by the Inquisition.

Sunsets? she wrote.

Intrigued, she skipped to the next promising one: a long snippet a few days ahead. Again, there she was on the cracked roads. This time it was evening, and she was walking slowly, dragging something heavy behind her. She looked back: it was a load of wood and metal, and tied to them in sacks, food supplies. It must have been tremendously heavy: the bots could all pull slightly more than an average adult human, and to slow down this way was unprecedented.

In a distance, the boy-bot. He was scouting ahead, spear in hand. He doubled back, metal glinting off his shoulders and knuckles, and started pulling with her.

Skip scene. They were eating by the light of a fading bulb. Her food disappeared quickly: very likely the cause of the phenomenal energy debt brought about by pulling that heavy load.

The boy looked over at here and offered half his food.

It was probably nothing complex on his part: a tribal energy-sharing mechanism, perhaps, weighted to keep all members of a unit functional. After all, he was from the Colombo 01 Zone, and built to foster relationships.

But the girl was not. She should have been feral and self-serving. Instead, Almeida watched as the video shook itself – the girl shaking her head – and then she went back and rummaged through the pile and pulled out more soya; and instead of serving herself first, she topped up the boy's bowl.

Unreasonable reciprocation. Kindness.

Attachment.

There were more. Feeling the sudden thrill of discovery, she rifled through the videos, aided by the object-counting program. Here was deduction of a lie: one of the people at the Port City's food serving line tried to tell her that they were out of food, and she insisted: the radio that she held played 'You have more.' until, grudgingly, they served up what they had.

And here was a solemn scene. A bot, caged, in a great, empty hall that spoke of opulence and grandness long since dead. Around the bot was a circle of bots, all children with a purple mark on their foreheads.

The Sons of Cinnamon.

A crystal chandelier, encrusted with bird droppings and dust, hung above, tinkling gently.

The bot tried to plead, crying its Prime Directive over and over again: *I want to live! Live!* Outside its cage, in the dust, were the bodies of three purple-marked bots: they would have looked for all the world like children resting, had it not been for the ghoulish holes in their chests.

The Sons looked to her, to Silent girl.

I want to live! cried the caged bot.

She shook her head. Hefted her spear. Pointed once at the dead bots on the ground, then at the cage. And with a casual throw, she sent the spear crashing through the cage, striking the caged bot through the head. It fell.

The other bots responded in kind, hooting gleefully, sending their spears through the cage until the bot stood pierced like a human pincushion. Silent girl shook her head and walked away.

In her office, Almeida sat back, stunned.

A trial. A court. Not what they had done to Aritha Bandara, but not far removed; the same principle, except a thousand years of civilization apart. Proof, blame, execution.

≈

'This is serious,' said Hewage when she showed this to him.

'I know!' she said, grinning,

Hewage did not seem to share her excitement. He doodled on the notebook, his brow furrowed.

'Sunsets, kindness, lie detection, trials,' he murmured, drawing lines between them. 'Bloody hell. The ultimate values.'

'Come again?'

He turned the notebook to her. 'Did they teach you the Greek values in university?'

'Democracy, men in togas and economic collapse?'

'Smart. Real smart. Listen carefully. There were four main things that the ancients considered essential to a human being. Beauty, goodness, truth and justice. It wasn't just the Greeks: the same ideals show up all over ancient history, right from the Hindu Bahgvad Gita. Plato goes on and on about this crap in Phaedrus.'

'Right, and?'

'Sunsets, kindness, lie detection, trials and execution. Beauty, goodness, truth and justice. You see the parallel? If you believe buggers who died a few thousand years ago, we've got the four main attributes of a human right here.'

She could barely contain her excitement this time. 'I told you! I told you these things could be alive in some sense! You never listened!'

Several people at the the nearby table paused their chatter and gave them odd looks.

'Idiot. Keep your voice down. We can't claim life based on what the Greeks said, that would be ridiculous. These were the same people who ran an economy off slaves and called it a democracy.'

'A lot of people still do.'

He brushed it aside. 'Ignore that crap. Point is you can't make an argument on bots using logic they used a few thousand years ago.' He doodled a bit more, thinking. 'You'll have to study that footage. Frame by frame, if possible. Observe. Correlate...'

'So what do we do? Whom do we tell?'

He lit a cigarette. 'Nothing. For now, you can't go around saying these things are alive.'

'But if they are...'

'Hypothetically. If they are, they've been for a while, so a little bit more won't hurt. In any case this girl could be an anomaly. Science. Facts. Build up a case. Watch that footage. Bring in more bots. Maybe build some more like that girl, put them out in the field. Build the correlations. It'll take years. And even then, people might not pay attention to you.'

He thought about it some more, taking long, slow drags on his cigarette. 'I'm certainly not going to do anything until I'm out of here. After you're Zone Controller. It can be your pet project,' he said. 'I'm not going to back a losing horse. You're smart, and your heart's in the right place, and you have all the data access you need. Prove it beyond doubt, and let's see what we can do without getting our hands burned. No guarantees. This is hypothetical stuff. I'm not going to lose a paycheck over it.'

'You do realize,' she said, stung, 'That if these things are alive, then we're torturing living things for entertainment?'

He looked at her as if she was mad. 'That's what we've always done. Gladiators. Slaves. How is this any different? The real question is, how are you going to prove it?'

TWENTY

Many years later, a young lawyer named Eraj Ekanayake stood ready to leave the office. It was Friday night, and all lawyers knew what that meant: more work over the weekend.

He had his foot halfway out of the office when Hilmy barelled out of his office and down the isle.

'I want you to take the Almeida case.'

'I don't want to take the Almeida case.'

Hilmy threw the folder. Eraj caught it out of reflex.

'You and I both know the Almeida case is a dud,' Eraj protested. 'We don't have half a chance of winning this. We're going to end up looking like fools in court for even taking it.'

'Not everything is about winning,' said Hilmy.

Eraj, frustrated, grabbed the folder and left, slamming the door on the way out. The Almeida case. A career-killer if he ever saw one. Nobody in their right mind would take the case: in fact, he had a sneaking suspicion Hilmy had passed it to him precisely because the others had turned him down. He was the youngest in the firm and thus the only person who couldn't tell Hilmy outright to fuck off.

≈

Which was how he ended up, two days later, at dinner with Dr Kushlani de Almeida, government employee, former Zone Controller for the Ministry of Reconciliation, and, in his mind, certified crackpot.

They met in one of the new high-rise hotels; Kandy had finally relaxed its height laws, and the Peacock, as it was called, was perhaps the finest result: a lush green-and-blue spiral that erupted from the earth, balconies spread out like the tips of feathers, looking out over the grim expanse of Kandy and its once-green gills: a jewel of color and noise in a land where so much had faded to dull gray.

He had never been here before, of course; all one could do on his salary was admire the Peacock from the tops of lesser hotels, the ones without the fancy climate-control fields, where the arrack tasted of acid rain and was twice as potent.

She was on time, of course, and he was late. She wore a black sari, austere and forbidding despite the silver fringes: a thick braid of salt-and-pepper hair coiled around her neck. He adjusted his tie, feeling suddenly self-conscious of the fact that he was five minutes late, and that he'd expected some kind of elderly matron with a hint of dotage. This woman looked more imposing than most men he knew.

'Sit,' she declared imperiously. 'Hilmy sent you? Has he finally run out of people?'

He ignored the jab. 'Eraj Ekanayake, Mrs Almeida,' he said, scooting into the chair. 'Sorry for the delay...'

'Miss.'

Whoops. 'Errrr... Nice evening, isn't it?' he tried.

She looked out over the gray skies and ruined earth, and the lake that cut through the landscape, as black as night.

'Yes,' she said. 'We'll need to wait for one more person. You can order.'

The waiter, as if summoned by magic, appeared with an expensive-looking menu and a smirk.

This was not off to a good start.

≈

The 'one more' turned out to be an old man with a cropped shock of white hair: he moved slowly, and Eraj was sure he could hear the voice of servomotors from his legs.

He also looked vaguely familiar. Eraj studied him as the man as approached. His wasn't one of those generic faces: this man had a lean face with a bitter twist to his mouth. It was a face that he had seen not too long ago...

Ah.

The Secretary to the Minister of Reconciliation. He had heard the rumours, of course.

'Ekanayake?' he said without preamble. 'Good. I asked Hilmy for his best.' The Secretary shot a glance at Almeida.

'Pleasure to meet you, sir,' said Eraj'

They settled in and the small talk began. Eraj relaxed, feeling steadily more relieved. It was almost a matter of routine. Family roots. Where he had gone to school, and with whom. The pedigree. The old 'Ah, I remember when...' exchange of two Ceylonese finding some common ground. It was easy: after all, this was Kandy, where everyone knew you, or knew someone you were related.

Kushlani de Almeida did not talk much. The soups arrived, and she dug into hers in silence. The Secretary regaled Eraj with tales from the Zone – including, for example, the notorious Aritha Bandara case.

After a while, she gave them both a look, as if she was saying *get it over with.*

And as the desserts arrived, it was time to talk in earnest.

'So,' said Almeida, swirling her wine glass. 'How much do you know about our case?'

Yikes. He hadn't read Hilmy's folder yet. 'Well, I've of course studied your argument that, uh, the machines that we use in the Entertainment Zone might actually be as self-aware as you and I...'

'And the counterargument, the one given by the government's roboticians?'

This he genuinely did not know. 'Erm. I read the argument about them being able to recognize beauty and truth...'

'So you know nothing useful, then. Hilmy's given up, hasn't he?'

'I don't know about Mr Hilmy, but this is how I approach all my cases, ma'am,' he found himself saying. 'Give me enough time and I'll know as much as you do.'

'You'll need thirty years, several degrees and a lot more brainpower than you have right now to know as much as I do,' she said. 'I'll settle for you knowing as much as the idiots facing us. I'm sending you my research brief.'

Eraj felt the hot flush on his collar. 'I'll have it memorized by the morning.'

She raised an eyebrow. 'A man with targets. Here.'

His phone beeped. Ten new files received.

She gave him that look again, and he understood he was being dismissed.

≈

They watched the young lawyer bumble his way out of the room. Hewage groaned.

'You shouldn't have done that,' he protested. 'I was warming up the lad nicely.'

Almeida smirked. 'Men are more predictable than our bots,' she said. 'He's young and he's still out to prove himself. I've lit a fire under his ass. Now he'll give us results.'

'You've spent too long in the Zone. You don't need to go around manipulating everyone just because you can.'

'Look who's talking.'

Hewage shrugged. 'Well, you have a point. But I try to play nice first. So are we still planning for...'

'If we don't win in court? Yes.'

'Of course you're not going to win. You want to tell hundreds of thousands of people that everything they've been doing for the last hundred years is wrong and you expect them to listen,' he snorted. 'You do realize that we have absolutely no idea what might happen if you go to Plan B?'

After that, for a while they ate in silence.

'How's the family?' she asked at last.

'The wife still won't let me visit my kid,' he said. 'Frankly, I'm not sure they want me back, either. I don't think anybody needs me anymore. Except your stupid crusade.'

'It's something,' she said.

'So much for goodness and truth all that crap,' he said. 'There's none left for us.'

≈

Eraj, still fuming, made his way out of the hotel. The cab, white against the bleak black and gray landscape outside, crawled up the kerb, and took him away from the blasted Peacock and Kushlani de Almeida.

He almost gave his home address, but changed his mind. 'Hilmy and Cader, Lawyers,' he said. 'Hill street.'

He brooded as the cab bounced softly onto the asphalt and joined the thin trickle of traffic heading up at this hour.

Damned stupid woman. Damned Hilmy. This case was a dud: he knew it, everybody knew it. The newspapers might run crap about prominent scientists claiming the bots were alive, but they all knew the only reason this was in courts in the first place was because the Mahanayake called for an investigation and the Inquisition was always happy to keep the Bandara entertainment complex in check. These were just stones thrown every so often to make sure the other side didn't relax too often. Games of chess.

And thanks to bloody Hilmy, Eraj was now a pawn. The case would sink catastrophically and put a large dent in everything he'd worked so hard for.

The taxi deposited him outside the office. Only one office had its lights on: Angela's. Probably the only person who had it worse than he did.

A light drizzle was falling, sending the familiar smell of sulphur up his nose.

Damned Hilmy.

Once back in his own office, he poured himself some tea and started reading. If Kushlani de Almeida was right about one thing, it was that he needed to know as much as the defendants. In this case, the defendent was the government.

1: Truth, beauty, justice, goodness: a philosophical bridge between artificial constructs and humanity

Right, so that was the one the papers were harping over. Plato and all that. Old Greek ideals for humanity.

But that one had been debunked in the papers: it would never hold water in court. All it had taken was for just one journalist to point out that the same Greeks who set these ideals also forbade women to vote. There is no justice, the *Times* had said, quoting the great Pratchett, there is just us.

2. Correlations: human behaviour compared to general prototype #3531

A lot of photos and annotations. It looked promising. More to the point, it looked readable.

He started reading.

'Okay,' he said a few days later, sliding into his seat. 'So I've read the files, and here's how it will probably go.'

De Almedia said nothing: she simply sat in Eraj's tiny little office and looked around with some curiosity at the neat stacks of records and indictments. He took this as a good sign and launched into his explanation immediately.

'I've looked at all of the arguments you've made, and the core of them is that technologically, these bots are essentially learning machines that, if given enough time without being reset, start showing extremely human-like behaviour. The logical argument is, if it walks like a duck, and starts talking and acting like a duck, then maybe we should treat it as a duck. Correct?'

'Reasonably accurate,' she allowed.

'Rght. Right. But you have to remember that we're essentially dealing with laymen! Human laymen,' he said. He was up now, pacing as he always did when explaining a case. So the first order of business is to start pointing out how similar they are, physically. Arms. Legs. Basic design. How the brain is designed. We present an argument that this thing is physically a metal human, because we designed it that way.'

'The brain doesn't exactly work the same way ours does,' she said. 'Which is precisely why I've had to spend years gathering evidence just to confirm my own hypothesis.'

'We don't tell them that. We leave it to the physicalities, which are obvious. We basically get Expert Witnesses out there to testify that yes, we've built metal children, and we put them to starve and fight each other for our entertainment. The judge might be the Mahanayake, but he's human. The jury is definitely human. We ask them how they would feel if their children were put to fight and die for entertainment, and we broadcast some of the most realistic snippets of the footage we can find.'

'Emotional manipulation.'

'It's a court of law. Humans have emotions, we might as well use them to our advantage. Because this'll set the stage for what happens next.' He thought fast, barely conscious of the little office, the smell of sulphur in the air. 'The opposition has one obvious card to play in response, and it's going to be: they are machines. We created them. They're not alive. We programmed those emotions into them.'

'To which we do two things. One, we bring an expert to explain the brain bits that you talk about, that it's a black box model, we don't actually program emotion, et cetera, et cetera. They learn from their environment. And we ask him, doctor, isn't that a lot like how a human child learns? I want him to say yes. So we've started off by making the opposition look dumb.

'Then we trip them up. We set up some bait. We ask the jury what it is to be human.' He gestured. 'The Platonic arguments, yes. But there are others. What else defines being human?'

She thought about it. 'Pain. Suffering.'

'Good, a Buddhist viewpoint. What else? Being born. Reproducing. Caring for children.'

'Energy consumption. Growth.'

'Empathy. Ambition.'

'One is emotional responses to others like ourselves. The other is basically ideation, planning and execution. We're also the only race to invent lawyers.'

He ignored the snub. She continued, 'You could even include the seven deadly sins in there.'

'Which are...'

'Pride, Gluttony, Lust, Greed, Wrath, Envy, Sloth... All fundamentally human attributes.'

'Right. And...um, Shakespeare.' He snapped his fingers impatiently. 'Hath not a man eyes? Organs? Dimensions? If you cut him, does he not bleed? So the physical stuff is the most obvious. People die. Mortality.'

'Robots die. Everything that has a beginning has an end.'

'My point exactly, Miss. We're trying to get them to see the parallels. If they bring out any of these arguments, we try to break them. We create reasonable doubt in the eyes of the judge and jury. We're not trying to prove sentience: we're trying to prove humanity.'

An eyebrow rose. 'I thought the whole point was to prove that they're sentient?'

'No, hear me out,' he said. 'The judge is human. The jury is human. We might have the most self-aware machine on our hands, but unless they can relate to it, nothing of what you want is going to happen. This is how humans work. How do we know we're sentient anyway? I'm sure you, like me, grew up looking at the world and wondering if everyone else saw through their own eyes the way you did. If you were the only real person around. Eventually, you learned enough about the others that you decided okay, they're as human as me. What's the base criteria here? *They are like me*. That's what we want to gun for.

'The other stuff like sentience is just too abstract. We can't swing a judge that way. These guys are going to be in that courtroom, and there's a fair bit of political pressure, and the media, and a bunch of people they really don't want to look like idiots in front of, so the easier we make it for them, the easier it gets for us. We don't need them to appreciate the inner workings of your robot brain. That can come much later. We just need to get them considered as living creatures that are kind of very, very human, hopefully too human to be used as entertainment all the time.'

'Hilmy did say you were talented,' she allowed.

A sip of water. There was that half-burned tinge in his throat, the one you got when there was a sore throat coming. 'But that's the second act. Third act is going to be stronger. We're going to relate it to the Civil Rights Movement of the black people of the American Colonies.'

'Oh?'

'And the Irish in England, I think. What they fought for was to stop being treated as slaves and start being treated as human citizens, right? So what are bots and AI if not the slaves of today? What are slaves if not just a primitive method of automation? So we have a precedent, and it's a precedent recognized throughout the Commonwealth, which makes it pretty important. If we can say, 'well, your honor, hundreds of years ago, people thought black men couldn't feel or were sub-human, and look what happened there. The prosecution today is behaving in exactly the same way the slave-traders did so many years ago. Big finisher. Very strong finisher.'

'Devious.'

He laughed. He had a short, barking laugh. 'Charmed.'

'Are you a Buddhist, Mr Ekanayake?'

'From my father's side, yes. My mother's Catholic.'

'That must have made an uncomfortable childhood.'

Another sip, not really thinking about the question, but Structuring and restructuring the case in his mind. 'She was English,' he said absently. 'Not many are going to protest about people who could blast us out of the water any day. But I still had to learn how to argue.'

'Interesting,' she said, rising, wrapping her saree's folds around her. 'There's one other argument that could be made, if you were arguing in a Catholic court: if God made Man in His image, and if we made the bots in our image, by inference, are they not also built in God's image?'

He thought about it and whistled, surprised. 'You'd have done well as a lawyer, Miss De Almeida.'

It was the only time he ever saw her smile, and for a moment something curious happened: it was as if the years fell away from her face, and instead of a gray, lined scientist at the end of her tether, there stood before him someone much younger and more radiant. 'Only in a courtroom run by machines, Mr Ekanayake.'

TWENTY-ONE

The courtrooms were filled; the balconies above crammed with journalists, shotgun microphones carefully aimed and calibrated. The defendant was Leslie Ekanayake: no relation; a name that, like his, had once been a common title – *Master of One*. Leslie was known for her formidable intelligence, her very pro-British views, and that made her a hard woman for the Great Families to control: rumor had it that she had a mansion tucked away in England. Not for the first time, he wondered what they'd given her to take the case. Certainly not money. A House sigil of her own?

The judge, the shaven-headed Mahanayake of Kandy, sat with his eyes half-closed, as still as a rock amidst the waves. The jury, a sea of orange robes, mimicked him, with varying degrees of success: they were young monks, most of them, picked for their anonymity.

He slid his eyes over the assembly. People. Faces. Flashing lights. Journalists.

And there. The black robes of the Inquisition. They stared at the judge and jury out of eyes that were ruby lenses, every so often shifting a shoulder that shouldn't have been there, or wiping away sweat with a hand that seemed attached at entirely the wrong angle, and altogether too machine-like.

Eraj felt marginally safer than he had expected to be.

The first half went exactly as he had called it. Leslie Ekanayake didn't dare call De Almeida an idiot outright: instead, she painted her as an academic perhaps a little bit more obsessed with the machines than was altogether too healthy. And, to the jury, she brought up the photos of that fateful shooting that had set all of this in motion: the little girl-bot and the boy-bot, skins suspended over grinning metal frames, dead in a pool of blood and lead. These were death machines, she said – emphasis on the machines – built by us for combat and sport: not only slaves to programming, but dangerous ones.

Perfect.

He could have asked for no better beginning. Eraj rose to his feet, adrenaline and the thrill of debate turning his usual bumbling awkwardness into Machiavellian precision.

'Your Honor,' he said. 'My colleague on the defending line made a fantastic point. I'd like to show you the video of that same scene: the one where the two bots were stopped by our fine police.'

And it played, and the buzz of the court fell into a deadly hush. He watched the faces of the jury as they saw the boy blaring, robot-voice Sinhala-Tamil stretched in what was clearly a scream, trying to crawl away as great chunks were ripped out of his chest. As they saw the girl, a tiny thing, confused and disoriented, bending over the boy's body, trying to shield him from the men with guns. They saw her shake her head, trying to hide, trying to plead.

They shot her. Once. Twice. Three times. She dropped the spear and tried to hold her palms out to them.

Four. Five. Six.

The body folded over the ruined carcass of the boy, still protecting him, even in death.

The jury of monks was unsettled. They had just seen the murder of two children. Excellent. He had gone to great lengths to procure that video and add it as evidence.

Eraj began to summon the witnesses, moving swiftly, his mind running to the beat Hilmy had drummed into him for years. *People like stories. Build a story. Beginning, middle, end.*

The first Expert Witness was Sir Rupert Crofton, of the Crofton Institute. Eraj had spent enormous sums of time and money looking for a British expert who would respect a colonial court of law enough to be grilled by Sri Lankan lawyers. Britain had a fantastic machine industry: indeed, the unwavering loyalty of Her Majesty's Tin Soldiers were legendary; but the second ask was tougher than the first. There were perhaps three people willing to admit that the Sri Lankan machine workshops had produced something worth investigating, and two of them had not answered his calls. Fortunately, Crofton was a much more approachable soul.

'Would you introduce yourself to the assembly, Sir Rupert?' he asked, approaching him with some deference.

'Certainly, my boy,' said Crofton, with that magnanimous benevolence used by the white man on the dark. He had a fantastic baritone voice that carried well: another reason for Eraj to bring him up first, before everyone became overloaded with information. 'Doctor Rupert Crofton, Machine Scientist to Her Majesty, at your service. I'm afraid the knighthood is still new.'

'Sir Rupert, would you describe yourself as an expert in the arts of the machine workshop?'

'Well, I should certainly hope so: the rest of the world does,' Crofton said with a chuckle. 'I did design most of the underlying logic systems for today's machines, if you must know.'

He had run Crofton through the basics before. The man knew his game.

'And what do you, Sir, make of this situation?'

Crofton slid his thumb up his nose, like a man absent-mindedly pushing up spectacles that weren't there anymore.

'Well, after careful analysis,' he said ponderously. 'It would appear that your Ministry of Reconciliation built a type of robot, which I believe is based on an Excelsior Type-14 system, with some fantastically new learning capabilities. I have to say it's caused quite a stir in the industry overseas, now that this has been brought to our attention. It would seem that this breed of bots, if left to learn for long enough, develops surprisingly human-like behaviours in their responses to the world at large. I believe you use these for entertainment, like the Gladiator matches of New Rome? Bots versus bots, except more gang violence than the usual sparring?'

'How human would you say is human, Sir Rupert?'

'Well, that's a difficult question, you understand. I'm not a philosopher-'

'From a technical perspective? From a scientist's perspective?'

'Aha. The bot has arms, legs, a head, a spine, just like a human. A brain houses the bulk of the intelligence, just like a human. And the software that runs this particular type of brain is very closely modelled on how we humans learn – we observe the world, identify patterns, and respond accordingly. Does it reproduce? Is it flesh? No, not really. But since these bots are trained for self-preservation, and to build group, I'd say from a very high perspective, the group behaviour of these bots are not really that different from what primitive Homo Sapiens might have exhibited. Tool-making, communication, self-organizing social circles, all of these are there. Which I assume is the point: realism for entertainment?'

Gold. 'So, to iterate what you just said – the behaviour of these bots approximates that of modern humans?'

'Modern primitive humans, yes. Old tribal societies.'

Score. He could push this. 'And what would you say of Dr De Almeida's findings, that individual bots also come to exhibit human characteristics?

That stumped him for a bit. 'I don't wish to speak ill of our colleague Dr. Kushlani De Almeida, but perhaps some conclusions are leaps of faith here. If I understand correctly, mimicry of human behaviour is precisely what these bots are designed for. These are black box models, you understand. Whether the bot evolves to express these behaviours, or whether they are ingrained as part of the testing process, is the important problem here.'

Shit. 'And how do humans learn these behaviours, Sir?'

'Nature and nurture, the biologists tell us. Social rulesets imposed at various ages, conditioning through interactions...'

'Could we equate, in the context of these machines,' said Eraj, 'That the training process could be considered "nature" and their life in the arena to be the "nurture"?'

Crofton thought. 'Yes.'

Recovery. 'At their current state, would you say they exhibit human behaviours at an individual level?'

'Judging from the evidence, definitely. Yes. Not all human behaviours, but certainly some.'

'And if these bots were not made of metal, but flesh, would you yourself see them as human?'

'I don't see why not. In a limited sense. Yes, I suppose I would, but I would still be aware that we, that is to say we humans, made these things, so in a sense I think most people would treat them like they belonged to us.'

'Like parents treat their children.'

'In a much more demeaning sense, I'd say, but yes.'

'So humanity, would you say, is a function of how people behave, instead of what they are made of?'

'Objection, *hamudhuruwane*!' barked Leslie, shooting to her feet. 'Leading the witness!'

'Noted, but continue,' said the Mahanayake. His voice was placid, but Eraj could see the interest building now. It was working.

Crofton noted this with interest and bent his mind to the question. They could almost hear the gears turning in the man's head.

'Well,' he said. 'What we generally consider human is someone who is flesh and blood. But there are certainly many of flesh and blood who no man in their right mind would consider human. The German atrocities, for example, or the cannibals of the Africas. And every religion and code of law in the world – forgive me if I misinterpret Buddhism, your Honor – assigns rights and privileges based on behaviour, not on bodily composition, at least to my understanding. We certainly treat rapists and murderers like the brutes they are. So it would follow, based on the context of the world we live in, that humanity is indeed a thing of behaviours.'

'And if a robot were to exhibit such all acceptable, human-like behaviours, that, say, you and I and this assembly would be capable of?'

Crofton looked around in astonishment. 'All behaviours you and I are capable of expressing?' he said. 'Why, I'd hang up my hat and shake its hand, of course. You'd have made life, man! A real human!'

He saw the heads nodding, especially among the lawyers in attendance. Even Leslie Ekanayake couldn't have done that better.

That was the easy part.

≈

Now it was up to Leslie Ekanayake, and Eraj knew there were two ways this could go. If Leslie had his measure, she would steer the case away from philosophy and into practicalities. If Leslie underestimated him, she'd stay in this realm.

Leslie Ekanayake threw philosophy at him. And the courtroom pivoted for Eraj, turning into a rapidfire hell where he could do nothing but break, break and break all points as they came; but it was an easier dance for him than Leslie knew. Not for nothing had Eraj spent days practising with Kushlani de Almeida.

'What makes a human? What makes life? People eat,' said Leslie Ekanayake. 'People grow and reproduce. Robots do not. Hamudhuruwane – your honor – and members of the jury – do you see how ridiculous this is?'

'Fire consumes, fire grows, fire spreads and reproduces,' Eraj shot back, his mouth spinning the words before he was even half aware of them. 'H*amudhuruwane,* the opposition's definition of life needs rethinking.'

'Machines are code that we've written!' thundered Leslie. 'Humans are of flesh. Humans are born from mothers' wombs.'

'What is a robot?' Eraj threw back. 'There are people in the audience who have been born in test tubes, who had body parts replaced with artificial organs. Are you calling them robots?'

He called up the next witness, a legislator; a retired lawyer and a second-tier politician. Really just a crutch piece: he had looked for the most literal-minded person he could find.

'Imagine that you are born a human,' said Eraj, pacing now, the tight, formal leather of his shoes cutting into his flesh inside. 'Imagine that you develop so many diseases that you end up replacing every single part of your body with a machine part. Are you, then, a robot? Should we put you in the Zone?'

Two things happened. In the benches, an Inquisitor shifted, dead eyes snapping to Eraj, who suddenly found himself sweating.

'Hamudhurwane, objection, out of bounds,' shouted Leslie. 'We're off topic!'

The Mahanayake waved her into silence. 'Answer, please,' he said to the witness in a dry husk of a voice.

'Well,' said the witness, who was old and perhaps too blind to see the Inquisitors. 'Common law does not exist for such detailed cases – remember, our citizenship laws are still what we had in the late 2000s. But to the best of my knowledge, the law of the country states that if a person is born within this country, they are to be treated as as a Sri Lankan citizen, with full rights.'

'And if a person was born through artificial means?' pressed Eraj.

'The law makes no such distinction,' said the legislator, as Eraj knew she would. He waited for Leslie to question his last set-up. Looked straight at her, right through the gimlet eyes and into the questions lurking beneath. But Leslie looked at the Inquisitors, looked back and Eraj, and subtly shook her head.

Just as Hilmy had predicted, in their many, many practice runs last night.

'No further questions for the witness,' Eraj said. He held his palms up. Hide the trembling. His work was done. Sow doubt; enough to make the judge and jury question Leslie's line of attack, enough to set up a gray area. Tie the robots to the one thing a court would never touch.

The Inquisitors in the room.

≈

'So they found one of the other explorer models,' said Hewage, sliding out his phone.

They watched as, on-screen, black-armored figures with guns surrounded a little girl who hissed and spat defiantly, spear at the ready.

The guns fired, the body jerked, and all was still.

'At least we're making headway in here,' said Hewage, pocketing the phone and waving his unlit cigarette at the courtroom.

'We're not,' said Almeida morosely.

'The kid just gave them a good run for their money.'

'All he's doing is muddying the damn water,' she said.

Crofton's last statement kept running through her mind. *You'd have made life.*

The very thought that had been running through her head ever since the first time she'd seen the Zone broadcast up close and unfiltered, before the networks cut in with their special effects; the same thought she'd had every time she'd seen the bots cringe with fear, or cry with pain or anger: the very thought she'd dedicated her life to for thirty years, proving beyond a doubt that it was not just a thought, but reality. And all for what? For a jury? A judge? For the definition of life to be up for philosophical debates by overpaid lawyers and underpaid journalists?

She saw the black figures again, the flash, the little body jerking.

'Thirty bloody years and it comes down to getting a jury of idiots confused,' she muttered, suddenly very angry. She had been glad when the judge called a recess. For a brief moment she could escape the prying eyes and the madness and be alone with her thoughts for a while.

'Speak of the devil,' said Hewage.

Crofton, his ridiculously white suit flapping, was bounding up the steps towards them. Only an Englishman would wear white to a place where the land was gray and the sky stained everything else black.

'Miss de Almeida!' he shouted jovially. 'What a pleasure!'

She saw journalists turn in the distance, saw cameras snap, and gritted her teeth.

'Sir Rupert,' she said, bowing, hands folded.

Up close, he was ruddy, and wore a powerful perfume that drove away the stench of sulfur for a second. 'And Hewage, you old dog!'

Handshakes, laughs. She gathered that they had studied together at some point: and, judging by how Hewage leaned, his experience had been none too pleasant.

'Well, what a day, eh?' said Crofton, wiping his ample forehead with a handkerchief that appeared out of nowhere. 'Who'd have thought that the defining case for sentience could come from Ceylon, eh? When I read your letter from that lawyer chap, I thought it was some small error, some gimmick in the OS, but here we are! Having a proper, proper debate! I say, isn't this exciting, Hewage!'

'Quite,' murmured Hewage.

'And Miss De Almeida, of course, some very interesting data you've gathered here ... even though I myself might disagree with the conclusions ... pardon me, if you don't mind me asking, did you study under old Hewage here?'

'She was my assistant.'

'Ah, I knew I'd seen that style of thinking somewhere. Pity, Hewage, you should have stayed at the Academy, you might even have ended up working with me – eh, what?'

This comment was directed to a photographer, who raised his camera and said, 'Sir?'

Crofton squeezed them together. There was a flash. 'Make sure you get my name right!' he yelled at the departing photographer. 'Anyway – where were we? Miss de Almeida, might I invite you to present your research at the Royal Academy of Robotics? Granted, all your work is based on much, much older software than what we have standardized, but perhaps some of my colleagues would enjoy restarting the old debate of whether they're alive or not, you know.'

Debate. Hewage shot her a look. She gritted her teeth again. 'And what about you, Sir Rupert? Where do you stand on the issue?'

He gave her a look that was probably meant to be wise, but instead came off as slightly alarmed. 'Here's the thing,' he said in a hushed, conspiratorial tone; they found themselves leaning forward to catch his words. 'It doesn't matter what we think, does it? How do we define sentience?'

She made to answer, but he shushed her. 'The secret definition is *are they like us!*' he whispered. 'You know, the more like us someone is, the more we like to think of them as equal! We didn't give rights to the blacks for hundreds of years until the public was convinced that they were like *us!* We burned the Scots and the Irish even though we have the same skin! You think it matters what data we collect or how well we argue? Your robots, my robots are all going to be human only when the people have decided that they're like us. Skin, speech, culture, the works. You're a man of the world, Hewage, you know what I'm talking about. I'm sorry, Miss de Almeida, but I don't see that happening for the next hundred years. Until that robot of yours can sit down somewhere, have a conversation, and not be noticed for a stranger, we're out of luck. Until then, sub-human is what they are, and sub-human is what they'll stay. Don't quote me on that, of course. Mustn't hold such views. Scientists like us must be optimists in public.'

He eyed them as if he had just imparted a great secret.'Now, if you'll excuse me, I need to find a bathroom,' he said. 'What say we catch up when all this is over, eh?'

And he was off, his ridiculous white coat flapping against the gray of the steps and the sky. The crowd waiting below opened up and swallowed him.

Fortunately, the bell rang, summoning them back into court, and they were spared the sight of the white man charming the flock. Kushlani de Almeida, brow furrowed, made her way back to her seat, her heart pounding with slow dread. The courtroom was full of hushed whispers, and stares sunk like daggers into her back.

She did not have to wait long. The jury trundled out, boy-monks in orange affecting a dignity they did not yet possess. They bowed to the Mahanayake, who looked at them kindly, and with implacable wisdom, and pronounced their verdict.

Dismissed.

Dismissed! The Mahanayake stood in a rustle of robes, commanding silence. 'We, the Sangha, do not find enough evidence to consider these to be living creatures,' he intoned, his voice shifted between judgment and placid preaching. 'Observe, all assembled. One of the great truths of this world is that all living creatures are born, and die at the end of their allotted lifespan, and are reborn, as the Buddha Himself said. This is the law of the world.'

She buried her head in her hands. All this work, for this.

'These machines are neither born; nor do they die; and however much they mimic us, we conclude that this is simply an illusion. So to all assembled I say: as a mirror held up to a candle mimics the light, so it is with them; the mirror had no true flame, and nor do these machines. This we declare in the name of the Buddha, the Dhamma and the Sangha, the Triple Gem.'

Sadhu, sadhu, came ritual hushed acceptance, the same words they had spoken to the Buddha when he finished his sermons. *Sadhu.* Well, said, O holy man.

But the holy man was not yet done. 'Kushlani de Almeida , this was a good-intentioned but ultimately misguided attempt,' he intoned, his voice cutting the sound of the courtroom like a sharp knife, 'While the Buddha advocated compassion, we cannot ignore that she was the cause of much waste of public monies and the time of those involved. Henceworth she must never pursue this topic again, and to apply her mind elsewhere; there are matters much more pressing to this country than these illusions.'

There was laughter now, mingled with the whispers. She saw Eraj Ekanayake, head bowed, looking defeated, shaking hands with his opponent; he did not look at her.

Bile rose in her throat. She fled.

'You know the shitty thing?' said Hewage later, as she stood on the steps of the courtroom, trying not the vomit.

'Don't say it.'

He said it anyway. 'He might be right.'

'They're never going to be able to sit down here and have a conversation,' she said. 'That's like expecting a toddler to get write a program. That's like chaining up a dog and refusing to feed it until it starts talking in Sinhala.'

Hewage shrugged. 'These are big problems,' he said eventually. 'People like us shouldn't get involved in them.'

'People like us *are* involved, dammit, people like us are the ones who create these problems!'

'Not saying it's right,' he said. 'Just saying it as it is.'

She turned to him, eyes distant. 'You think karma will set things right? That there might actually be a reckoning due?'

He scoffed and lit his cigarette, taking long, deep puffs. 'Do I think there's some kind of cosmic equation that'll balance out everything that's happening?' he said. 'No, I don't. I'm going to get back to the lawyer, see what's happening there.'

'What do you believe in?'

'I think only people with power can do any damn thing in this world,' he said, starting down the steps. 'You can either do it, or you can't. Apply your mind elsewhere, like the monk said.'

She watched him go.

And she knew what she had to do.

TWENTY-TWO

It was night.

A pale and sickly moon hung over the darkness of Kandy, Ceylon. Spires, many of them new, gleaming hotels, reached out to the sky, strange snakes of metal reaching out to gray-black ink of clouds.

'THE BLUETOOTH DEVICE IS READY TO PAIR,' blared a voice in a distant part of the country, too far away for anyone to hear.

Dr Kushlani De Almeida travelled like a ghost in the darkness. A taxi brought her up to the driveway of the Ministry of Reconciliation, to the blasted tree that she had walked past many, many times before. As she shut the door, the taxi suffered a catastrophic failure from an unexplained electromagnetic pulse, wiping its memory and resetting it to factory defaults. It beeped twice, as if puzzled, and set off down to long route to the taxi company.

The Ministry of Reconciliation loomed, all concrete spires and glass. The door accepted her immediately. The guards, who on other occasions may have barred the door, saw her, looked at her badge, and waved her in, wondering what a cleaning lady was doing at this time.

'Probably left her mop behind,' joked one of them, and they turned back to their vigil.

The cleaning lady entered the lift and disappeared.

Ten minutes later, she was in the Zone Control office. The vast, circular broadcast station that she had inherited and eventually passed seemed to hum with promise in the darkness. Her fingers found the old, familiar keyboard, danced over it: in a second, lights were firing up, the wallscreens lighting up around her, switching from gray noise to the signal...

And there they were.

The Zone. The bots. Sleeping. Children tucked into the corners of ruins and carefully staged, carefully burnt vehicles, bodies in repair mode, lit by the same moon that hung over Kandy. Colombo 1. 3. 4. A few moved, moving in the darkness like cats on the prowl, always alert.

The system asked her for passwords: she typed in the old ones, the ones they had always meant to change, but never did. Moving quickly, she plugged in the drives she had brought.

It was the matter of minutes to trigger the update system, replace the new build with the files she had brought. It was a small update. Nothing as fancy as what had gone through her head for many years – such as recreating Silent girl, extracting her mental model, mapping that onto the new bots, somehow.

No, this was much simpler.

Commit update?

'Hands off the keyboard,' a voice rang through the darkness. 'Do it now or I shoot.'

Fear hit her like a train. She jumped, and found herself facing a gun barrel, glinting in the cold blue light; and on the other end of it, an old man, tall, and angular, and dressed in a dark suit and hat.

It had been years, but something about him was immediately familiar.

'You!'

The Chief Inquisitor of Kandy made a low bow with his head and gestured for her to move away from the terminal. 'I have to question what exactly you think you were doing, Miss Almeida,' he said. 'Is it a habit of yours, to break into Ministry premises in the dead of the night?'

'I thought you were dead! What the hell are you doing here?'

'Perks of having the Inquisition at your beck and call, Miss de Almeida,' the old man said, sketching a bow. 'I'm very much alive, as you can see. Perks of not being human enough to die, though I think you've started some debate on what that means. Did you really think the Ministry would go unguarded in some fashion? After all the public drama you've kicked up? My boys stationed here tell me they saw you entering the building disguised as cleaning staff, so I find myself having to meet you here at these unseemly hours.'

She edged slowly towards the trolley. Those bottles of bleach. She had taped a little vial of acid inside each one, just in case something happened. One good kick and the vial would shatter and a furious reaction would spew out chlorine gas, destroying eyes, lungs...

His face, gray and cold, pushed right up to her, pushing the gun right up to her throat. She shivered at the touch of the cold metal. Behind him, other shadows began to emerge: black-robed men, if they could be called men.

'I'm afraid they don't let me use use barbiturates in questioning anymore, so we'll have to do with the gun,' he said softly. 'So. I won't ask again. What exactly is it that you intended to do?'

There was nothing else she could do. She told him. The gun dug deeper into her neck.

'Five lines of code.'

She couldn't decide whether it was a question or statement. 'All it does is block the updates and the memory resets,' she said. 'The first bots grew because we couldn't update them when we needed them to fight and reset them when they died.'

He stared at her, unblinking. 'And the Zone, will they not see the updates failing to install?'

'It's just an acknowledgement signal from one end,' she said, aware that she was getting higher-pitched, sweating in the cold. 'Easy to fake.'

'And then what? Your robots become human, like Pinocchio? You think your courts will grant them rights after that?'

The shadows moved closer. An eye glinted in the darkness, all lenses and metal frames.

She panicked. 'No, they're not, but you have to understand – we need to give them time, and if we do, they *might*. Please – you have to understand – we treat them like scum, we made the next generation of humanity and we used them for entertainment – maybe they'll die, maybe they'll kill each other, but at least they'll have a chance...'

He sighed, pulled the gun away.

'A boy who won't be good might as well be made of wood,' he said, stepping back. 'Have you learned nothing from how you treat the Inquisitors? Come with us.'

The Inquisitors in the shadows moved towards her: one had handcuffs, dangling from what looked like a hand.

And Kushlani de Almeida gave the bleach bottles a good kick. She was confused, and she had no idea what the man was talking about, but she had been prepared for this.

She looked at the screen. Commit update? it asked of everyone and no one.

'Come,' repeated the Chief Inquisitor. 'Let's not make this unpleasant.'

Around the caps of the bottles, a gas began to form.

'Yes, yes, I'm sorry,' she said, daring to drop her hands, edging forward now. 'It won't happen again...'

She darted forward. Hit a key.

Update in progress.

'Well, shit,' said the Chief Inquisitor, and shot her. The bullet, and old-fashioned metal slug, left the chamber and entered her heart at the same moment that the first bleach bottle exploded, spewing toxic green fumes over everyone. The Inquisitors reeled, clawing at their eyes; those who had lungs doubled over, coughing.

All around Colombo, children woke up, their eyes the dull, unfocused stare of a robot receiving an update. As

Kushlani de Almeida fell, red blood black under the cold blue lights, the children of Colombo snapped awake.

Update applied.

EPILOGUE

Many years later, a man was being dragged through a dead, broken street. His captors clung to him with fists of iron, pulling him relentlessly forward, deaf to his pleas and cries of pain.

He stumbled, feet bleeding. He was supposed to be blindfolded, but the grimy cloth had slipped, and now he caught glimpses of crumbling concrete and cracked metal railings. Like himself, the world had seen better days.

Presently the rag was ripped from his face.

Three bots stood before him. One of them, a girl, held what looked like a metal shaft, wrapped around with cloth and barbed wire and something black that held the whole thing together. The others might have been of any gender once; now they were short, stocky creatures with skin stripped off their hands and faces so that they were grinning skulls of metal.

A boot planted itself in his back and kicked him, sprawling, to the ground before them.

'This one was outside,' one of his captors said, in that low, electronic guttural Sinhala-Tamil mix that the bots used.

One of the grinning bots moved as if to dispatch him. He cried out in fear. The girl stopped the bot, barbed metal shaft planted in its way.

'Maybe we should let it go,' she said.

'It is human,' said the other.

The girl crouched, peering at the pitiful human that cowered, wailing. 'Yes,' she said.

'It is human,' repeated the other, as if with disbelief.

She pried the human's hands away from his face with hands that could have crushed him into pulp. 'They have eyes,' she said. 'Look. They have have skin, feet, hands, like us. They are weak, but they bleed, laugh, cry. Look, the sun hurts them.'

'They kill us,' the other said, also crouching. 'Look, hands, can hold weapons. Eyes, can see us. Feet, can run from us.'

The human screamed and made incoherent noises.

The girl studied the human's bleeding, torn face one last time. 'Give this one food and water, and let it run into the jungle.'

She gave a signal, and iron hands clamped around the human and dragged him away.

'Foolish,' said her aide; his metal face-skull glinted blood-red with the light of the dying sun. 'It will lead the rest of the pack here. They will kill us all.'

'Maybe,' said the girl-bot gently. 'But if we kill them all, are we any better than them?'

To this the bots had no answer. They nodded in mute assent, logic acknowledging their leader's wisdom: and with one last look, they turned their back on the human settlement, and vanished into the evening.

ACKNOWLEDGEMENTS

I suppose this is where I thank everyone, starting with the cat.

In reality, the cat had nothing to do with it. Don't listen to his lies.

The Inhuman Race was written mostly in isolation. It emerged from under the shadow of my previous book like a weed, and like a weed it grew until it had taken over the garden, laid siege to the walls and sucked dry all the other story-plants I had potted. Much of the credit for making this book happen goes to Kanishka Gupta and Swati Daftuar. Kanishka, my superb agent, kept bugging me every week – "Book? BOOK?? BOOK??!" until I finished the thing, at which point he worked his magic and called me a week later with a four-book deal from HarperCollins. Swati, my editor, presumably filled in the rest of the mystical process by which an author ends up working with a publishing house – she took a risk on a complete stranger from Sri

Lanka, and before I knew it I was treading through her office trying to figure out how many of her books I could steal in one go.

The others who participated, willingly or not, can actually be counted on one hand. Navin, with who I debate science, Warhammer 40K and world history. Sajith, Lasantha, Dulitha and Yoshith, who by fairly winding journeys crossed my path and brought a bottle along with them. Professor Rohan Samarajiva, who asked some extraordinarily piercing questions that forced me to think harder about the world behind my book, and where it split from reality. And the good folks over at r/worldbuilding, with whom I once had a very informative debate about my fictional world.

Most important of all: philosopher John Searle and his 1980 paper Minds, Brains and Programs, which presented the Chinese Room thought experiment I have repurposed herein. Thought I have to say I disagree with its conclusion: I have thus subverted it here to argue against his original premise. The original exploration is worth reading, though, for any understanding of artificial intelligence: it's a thing of startling beauty, somewhat similar to Gottfried Leibniz's 1714 argument; I saw it, in a different form, in Peter Watts' Blindsight ...

Alright, this hand has at least ten fingers. I can probably fit it in the next book somewhere.

But I maintain that the cat did absolutely nothing. That's my story, and I'm sticking to it.